FINDING HOME

KATHRYN SPRINGER

CONTENTS

To every woman who was once a little girl who loved horses
(you know who you are!)

Trust in the Lord and do good; dwell in the land and enjoy safe pasture. Delight yourself in the Lord and he will give you the desires of your heart.

—Psalms 37: 3,4

"**W**hat do you mean there's a glitch? What kind of glitch? I'm supposed to sign the paperwork on Monday!"

Julia Windham rose to her feet so abruptly that the chair she'd been sitting on began to tip over. Her fingers curled around the wooden spindles—an attempt to steady not only the chair but the sudden, uneven skip of her heart.

"Please sit down, Julia. I'll try to explain what happened." The thread of tension in Lucy Robertson's cheerful, customer-friendly voice hinted that she wasn't looking forward to the task.

Julia's gaze shifted from the Realtor to the bay window over her kitchen sink instead. A skein of gray smoke unfurled from the stone chimney on the house across the pasture.

She turned accusing eyes on the woman seated at

the kitchen table. "Wait a minute. Are you telling me that the. . .*the glitch*. . .is there?"

In my house, she wanted to add.

The only thing that prevented her from saying the words out loud was the knowledge that the house didn't belong to her yet. But it would. By ten o'clock on Monday morning.

Glitch or no glitch.

When Lucy had called earlier that morning and asked if she could stop by for a few minutes, Julia had assumed it was to talk about the closing. She hadn't even thought it strange the Realtor had chosen a Saturday morning to go over the final details. The town of Jackson Lake, Wisconsin, was so small and full of down-home charm that it wasn't unusual for people to discuss business over a cup of coffee at Roscoe's diner rather than in an office building.

That cozy, everyone-knows-your-name way of life was one of the reasons Julia chose to live *outside* the city limits.

She took a restless lap around the room while she waited for Lucy to deny it.

Except that Lucy *didn't* deny it.

"I know this is going to come as bit of a shock, Julia." The Realtor sighed. "When you and I spoke on the phone after the attorney called and asked me to list the Kramer property, I had to go out of town for a few days. I left my. . .um, mother. . . in charge of things. I did mention that I'd hired her part-time, didn't I?"

2

"I think so." But if Julia wasn't mistaken, Irma's main duties involved answering the phone and scheduling an occasional showing. "But you told Irma that I'd already made a verbal commitment to buy the property, didn't you?"

The twin spots of color that tinted Lucy's cheeks answered the question. "I was only going to be gone a few days. I didn't think it was necessary to tell her that you've always had a standing interest in the Kramer place."

"And now someone else is interested."

Unfortunately, Lucy didn't deny that, either.

"The day after I left, someone called and said he was looking for a house in the country. I hadn't even bothered to log the property into the computer, but when Mom was still on the phone with him, she spotted the notes I'd jotted down. She saw a new listing and a potential buyer and decided it was. . ."

"A chance to prove herself." Julia finished the sentence when Lucy's voice trailed off.

"No." Lucy shifted uncomfortably in the chair. "Divine intervention."

"Divine intervention." Julia repeated the words in disbelief.

"You know Mom." The woman's shoulders lifted in a helpless shrug. "She doesn't believe in coincidences."

Julia wanted to argue that from where she stood, the situation seemed more like a cosmic joke than divine intervention. Especially given the fact that she and God hadn't been on speaking terms for a long time.

She couldn't believe this was happening. When Lucy had called with the news that Zach Kramer's only surviving relative had finally decided to sell the house next door, she'd been thrilled.

And now some. . .*outsider*. . .wanted to buy it.

What Julia couldn't figure out was why.

The acreage itself wasn't anything to get excited about—a small notch of land near the creek that bordered Julia's property. Tangled ropes of wild grapevine wove through the branches of the oak trees that circled the unkempt yard. The changing seasons had gradually taken their toll on the two-story house, whittling away at it until only a glimpse of its original charm remained.

Did the person interested in buying it want to turn the house into a weekend retreat? Or fix it up and resell it for a profit?

Neither possibility set well with Julia.

"The client drove up and took a look at it. . ." Lucy paused and a shiver of unease skated down Julia's spine.

Every time Lucy paused, the situation got more complicated. And Julia didn't like complicated.

She glanced out the window again. The smoke had drifted closer to Julia's house in a blatant disregard for property

lines.

"Irma gave him permission to spend the night

there?" she guessed. "Is that something you let prospective buyers do now? Try out the property before they buy it?"

"Prospective buyers, no." Lucy studied the lace tablecloth as if she'd never seen one before. "Buyers. . .yes. The paperwork was signed an hour before I got back into town late yesterday afternoon. The property officially belongs to a man named Cameron Delaney now."

———

"WIND RIVER FARM. Does our farm have a name, Dad? Can we give it one?"

Cam Delaney suppressed a smile as he turned down the paved driveway just beyond the weathered sign Beth had spotted. If he could only figure out a way to bottle and distribute his ten-year-old daughter's enthusiasm, he'd be a multimillionaire.

"I don't see why we can't. Although it's not really a farm."

"Not yet." Beth bounced on the seat, her lively gaze taking in the scenery around them. "But it will be."

"How about you and I move in first? Before we start collecting animals like Noah?"

"Or we could all move in at the same time."

"Come to think of it, the house does have a unique, *country* odor." Cam couldn't resist teasing her a little.

"The animals should feel right at home in our living room."

"The house smells great." Beth smiled blissfully, as if she'd spent the night in a four-star hotel rather than a drafty old house that creaked and shuddered every time the wind blew. "Everything is great. I can't wait for Granna Claire to see it. She's been praying that we would find just the right house. And we did."

Cam hoped his mother would feel the same way when she got her first glimpse of the place that Irma Robertson, the woman who had given them an official tour of the place, had cheerfully referred to as "a handyman's dream."

To most people, it probably looked more like a nightmare.

"Do you think Ms. Windham will like the brownies I made for her?"

Another bounce. Another question. He'd been peppered with them from the moment Beth poked her head out of the sleeping bag that morning. Only this time, Cam wasn't sure how to answer.

The garrulous Irma Robertson, who'd provided him with brief but thorough background information on most of the residents of Jackson Lake, had become strangely evasive when Cam had inquired about their closest neighbor. The only thing she'd said was that Julia Windham lived alone and "kept to herself."

Cam filled in the blanks, understanding it to mean that the elderly woman preferred to be left alone.

Unfortunately, it hadn't translated the same way to his outgoing daughter.

While Cam had spent the majority of the morning taking an inventory of the repairs the house would need, Beth had been busy, too.

She'd added a box of brownie mix to the cart when they'd made a quick trip into town to pick up a few groceries the night before. And his daughter had quickly set him straight about who was going to reap the fruit of her labor. When he reached for the pan cooling on the scarred countertop, she had informed him the brownies were for Ms. Windham.

A "welcome to the neighborhood" gift.

Cam didn't want to point out that since they were the ones who were new to the neighborhood, it made more sense that *they* be on the receiving end of dessert.

But he'd given in, because generosity—like flossing —was another important quality that Claire Delaney had encouraged in her granddaughter. It was up to him to keep the torch lit.

As a single dad, Cam had come to rely on his mother's wisdom and experience. She'd braved the shopping malls for school clothes in the fall and organized Beth's annual birthday parties. Her sense of humor and deep faith had helped smooth out the rough spots after Laurel died.

Cam had finally given up trying to repay his mother because he didn't think he could. The opportunity, however, had unexpectedly presented itself on

Christmas Eve. A widower named Robert Owens had been visiting their church and happened to sit next to them during the fellowship time after services.

Cam figured it was the first time in Claire Delaney's life that she had deliberately ignored someone. It was so out of character, Cam did what any good son would do for the mother who'd put her life on hold for eight years in order to make his a little easier.

He and Beth had invited Robert over for dinner.

Robert had accepted the invitation. And the next. In fact, the retired surgeon had wisely accepted every dinner invitation that followed until he'd won Claire over.

It hadn't taken long. A month ago, Cam had walked his mother down the aisle. Beth had been the maid of honor.

Before she'd left for her honeymoon cruise, Mom had ambushed him, suggesting that maybe it was time for him to make a new start, too. At first, Cam had rejected the advice.

A new start? He was doing fine. He and Beth were both doing fine.

But she'd made him promise that he would pray about it.

In a roundabout way, the answer to that prayer was the reason he and Beth had ended up trading a two-bedroom condo in the Windy City for a fixer-upper that looked as if it belonged on the set of *Green Acres*.

"Look at her barn!" Beth squealed. "It's huge."

From the expression on his daughter's face, Cam could tell she was trying to determine just how many horses a barn that size could hold.

As they pulled up to the house, the curtains in the window drifted shut. It occurred to Cam that maybe it wasn't such a good idea to drop in unannounced on an elderly woman who lived alone on an isolated country road.

"Beth, why don't we—" *Come back another time,* he was going to say. After they'd called first.

"Get the brownies, Dad!" His daughter had unbuckled her seat belt and was already scrambling out of the car.

By the time Cam had closed the car door, Beth was halfway up the flagstone walkway that led to the front door.

Because it was tucked away in the sheltering circle of a stand of oak trees, Cam hadn't realized the house was so big.

Or so imposing.

His gaze moved from the stately two-story brick home to the L-shaped barn farther down the driveway. Several outbuildings fanned out around it, all of them painted an identical shade of brick-red and trimmed in white. Empty flower boxes lined the multipaned windows of an oversize shed, ready for spring planting.

There was an understated elegance to everything. In fact, it looked more like a country estate than a farmhouse. And it was a far cry from the place that he and Beth were going to call home.

Cam resisted the sudden urge to check for a servants' entrance at the back.

By the time he reached Beth's side, she'd enthusiastically tried out the bronze door-knocker several times.

She frowned up at him. "I don't think anyone's home."

"That's all right." Cam tried to hide his relief. It was probably better this way. "We can leave the brownies on the porch with a note."

"But her dog might eat them."

"I didn't see a dog."

"Neither did I, but she has to have one. It's a farm, Dad."

Cam knew there was no point in arguing. Beth firmly believed that everyone who lived in the country would have as many animals as possible. Just because they could.

"Fine. I'll find a safe place for them while you run back to the car and write Ms. Windham a note. There's paper in the glove compartment."

Beth looked disappointed but darted back to the car to carry out her part of the mission.

While Cam tried to decide the best place to keep the pan of brownies away from a dog that may or may not exist, the front door opened.

A woman stepped onto the porch but she wasn't the elderly neighbor Cam was expecting to see.

Not even close.

This woman was in her mid-to-late twenties. Tall and slender with a cap of honey-blond hair that framed delicate features—sculpted cheekbones, a small, straight nose and a pair of stunning, violet-blue eyes.

Cam blinked.

Because the cool look in those stunning, violet-blue eyes made him sorry he *hadn't* checked for that servants' entrance.

"We're looking for Julia Windham. I'm Cam Delaney." He extended his hand. "My daughter, Beth, and I are moving into the house down the road. We wanted to stop by and introduce ourselves."

After a moment's hesitation, she touched her fingers to his in the barest of handshakes before quickly pulling her hand away.

"I'm Julia Windham."

Cam Delaney.

Moving into the house down the road.

Julia barely had time to connect those two shocking pieces of information when the petite, redheaded whirlwind she'd seen from the window skidded up to them.

"I'm Beth." The little girl grinned up at her. "We thought you'd be old. Dad and I were just about to leave the brownies on the porch. I didn't want to because I thought your dog might eat them. Chocolate isn't good for dogs, you know. Dad's a veterinarian so I know all kinds of things about animals. . ."

"Brownies?" Julia slipped in the question when Beth Delaney paused to take a breath. She was trying to make sense out of the "we thought you'd be old" comment when another one registered. "Dog? I don't have a dog."

Disappointment clouded Beth Delaney's big brown eyes for a moment. "Cats?" Her tone was hopeful.

"No. No cats, either." Julia fought the strangest urge to apologize.

"But you have horses, right? We saw the barn."

Julia sucked in a breath. Funny how one simple question possessed the power to pierce her defenses and scrape against a wound that had never completely healed.

She shook her head.

"But this is a farm." Beth looked confused. "I saw the sign by the driveway. Wind River Farm. All farms have animals. Dad said I could name our farm. . .unless it has a name already. Do you know if it has a name?"

Julia took a step backward. Toward the safety of the house. She shouldn't have answered the door. When she'd heard the car pull up and saw the little girl jump out of the passenger side, Julia had assumed she was involved in some sort of school fundraiser.

If she'd had any inkling the vehicle belonged to her new neighbors, she would have followed her first instinct and ignored the enthusiastic pounding on the front door.

Julia stole a glance at the girl's father and then quickly looked away.

She'd thought the situation with the house was a major complication but Cam Delaney could very well fall under a whole separate category.

They had expected her to be old? Well, the Delaneys

hadn't been the only ones guilty of making false assumptions.

Julia's imagination had created a picture of the man who had snapped up what was supposed to have been her land and it had been what the locals referred to as a "weekend warrior." A middle-aged man in denim and flannel, holding a chainsaw in one hand and a fishing pole in the other.

Cam Delaney, with his tousled sable-brown hair, jade-green eyes and ruggedly masculine features, fit the warrior part of the equation, at least.

That was what was so unsettling.

Not only was he attractive enough to grace the cover of an outdoor magazine, he exuded the casual aura of a man who didn't seem to realize it. If someone found that appealing. Which Julia didn't.

"Does our farm have a name?" Beth repeated the question, tilting her head in a curious way that reminded Julia of the chickadees that visited the bird feeder outside her kitchen window every morning.

"I don't think so," Julia murmured. "Everyone around here calls it the old Kramer place."

Beth wrinkled her nose. "It's too pretty for that name. After Dad and I fix it up it'll look even better. We stayed there last night, and next Saturday we're going to bring the rest of our stuff."

"You're going to *live* there?" The words spilled out before Julia could stop them and her eyes flew to the girl's father. "I thought. . .when Lucy Robertson said

14

you were from Chicago, I assumed you would be spending weekends there. Or maybe fixing it up in order to resell it."

"No—we're here for the long haul." Cam Delaney sounded way too cheerful about it. "I accepted a partnership with Dr. Blake."

"I see." Julia braced one hand against the doorjamb. She vaguely remembered hearing a rumor that Thomas Blake, the small-animal vet, was planning to retire soon, but most people had assumed his son would return to Jackson Lake and take over his practice.

"The house needs a little bit of work but Tig and I are up to the challenge, aren't we?" Cam reached out and gave one of his daughter's copper braids an affectionate tug.

"Dad! I told you not to call me that anymore." Beth's slim shoulders rolled in time with a long-suffering sigh. She gave Julia an apologetic look. "Dad says I remind him of Tigger because I have a lot of energy. It's kind of a baby name, though, and I'll be eleven in a few weeks. I hope I get a puppy for my birthday."

Wonderful. Julia's lips tightened. With no fence between the two properties, their new pet would probably be a frequent visitor. Digging up her flower beds. Barking incessantly. . .

Her gaze suddenly collided with Cam Delaney's. His smile faded, the jade-green eyes darkening as if he'd read her thoughts.

Julia lifted her chin, forcing herself not to look

away. This was her porch. She wasn't the. . .the interloper here.

"Beth, why don't you give Ms. Windham the brownies?" Cam suggested softly. "I think we've taken up enough of her time. And we should be back on the road before dark."

"Okay." Beth flashed a sunny smile as she retrieved the pan from the porch rail and proudly presented a foil-wrapped plate, crowned with a topknot of yellow curling ribbon.

———

CAM'S BREATH stalled as Julia Windham stared at the plate in Beth's hands.

She was about to reject his daughter's gift.

Take it. Please.

He didn't know how Beth would handle the rejection. His baby girl had a tendency to see the good in everything. And everyone.

He, on the other hand, should have seen this coming.

Julia Windham's chilly demeanor hadn't thawed a bit since she'd stepped onto the porch. The expression on her face sure hadn't matched the word *Welcome* stamped in gold letters on the mat beneath her feet. If anything, she had become even more reserved after Beth had quizzed her about the pets she owned.

Just what he needed. A neighbor who didn't like children or animals.

Until now, Cam hadn't realized how much he'd hoped their "elderly neighbor" would become somewhat of a surrogate grandmother to Beth. Someone to fill the void of his mother's absence.

Okay, Lord. What's going on? Jackson Lake is great. The job looks promising. The house is everything we wanted. . .but Julia Windham as a neighbor? Sorry—I must be missing something here.

What kind of person turned down chocolate? Handmade by a cute little redheaded kid?

Cam saw Beth's smile falter and his heart slammed against his rib cage.

He was about to do damage control when Julia accepted the gift.

"Thank you." The words were polite, her smile looked forced. "Did your mother help you make them?"

"Nope. It's just me and Dad," Beth said matter-of-factly. "Granna Claire taught me how to bake. She said it takes two people to make enough cookies to satisfy Dad's sweet tooth—"

"Beth." Cam saw his daughter's eyes widen and realized he'd spoken more sharply than he had intended. But he doubted Julia was interested in the mundane details of his personal life. "It's time to go. We've got a few more things to do before we leave." He gently put his hands on her shoulders and directed her toward the car.

"Let me know if you like the brownies!" Beth slipped from his grasp and Cam knew what was about to happen. Unfortunately, he wasn't fast enough to prevent it.

His daughter was a hugger. No one was exempt. It was a gene she'd inherited from her mother, so Cam indulged the habit.

Until now.

"Beth—" He swiped at her sleeve and ended up with a fistful of air instead.

Beth's arms clamped around Julia's slim waist. "Thanks for having us over. We'll stay longer next time. Promise."

Julia stiffened and Cam wasn't sure if she was going to scream or shake his daughter off like a piece of tissue paper stuck to the bottom of her shoe. Or both.

"Thank you." Julia gave Beth's head an awkward pat instead. Once. Twice.

Beth released her with a grin. "It was nice to meet you. Bye!"

With a quick nod, Julia dove for the door. It slammed shut behind her.

"Come on, Tig." He reeled Beth in and gave her the kind of hug she deserved.

On the drive back to Chicago, Cam had time to think about Julia Windham. And the expression on her face before she'd disappeared into the house.

Given the woman's less-than-welcoming reception,

he had expected to see displeasure. Or impatience. But oddly enough, the emotion that skimmed through those incredible violet eyes had looked more like. . .pain.

"**G**o home, now. You aren't welcome here."

A pair of liquid-brown eyes stared sorrowfully at Julia over the heirloom rose-bush she'd been trimming.

"I mean it." She sat back on her heels and frowned at the un-invited guest. "I don't have time for company."

Aahroorooroo!

Julia dropped the pruning shears and clamped her hands over her ears.

The newest addition to the neighborhood—Cam Delaney's enormous mongrel of a dog—mistook the shooing motion she'd made with her hands for an invitation to play. As if the animal were hinged in the middle, the front end of its body dropped to the ground while the part with the tail remained in the air.

Two furry eyebrows twitched hopefully.

"You couldn't have been a Chihuahua, could you? Oh, no. They had to adopt the biggest—" Julia stopped herself from saying the word *ugliest* only because the poor animal had had no choice about its questionable pedigree. One part timber wolf and two parts polar bear. "*Loudest* dog they could find."

Not to mention the smelliest.

The plumed tail slashed the air and Julia reared back.

Ach.

The creature was shedding so much fur it looked as if they'd experienced a mid-April snowfall. Julia picked a rogue hair off her sweater and flicked it away.

"Where is your family, by the way? Shouldn't they be keeping a closer eye on you?" Once again, Julia found her gaze drifting to the house across the field. Something that was happening way too often as the day wore on. But who could blame her? The quiet country road she lived on had become Grand Central Station over the past few hours.

The traffic had started just before noon, when Cam Delaney's car had chugged past. Part of a caravan that included a moving truck and an apple green SUV with the Robertson Realty logo on the side.

Julia guessed that Lucy had stopped by to officially present Cam with the keys to the house that should have belonged to her.

While the movers began unloading all of Cam and Beth Delaney's worldly possessions, Tom Blake's pickup had pulled up. That's when the dog had made its first appearance.

She had assumed—*hoped like crazy*—the shaggy monster tearing around the yard belonged to Dr. Blake. But when the vet finally drove away, the dog had stayed. He'd either left it behind on purpose—and Julia wouldn't have blamed him a bit—or else Cam Delaney had decided to present his daughter with an early birthday present.

As if on cue, a flash of yellow caught Julia's eye. A small figure shot out the back door and ran around the house. Seconds later, a shrill whistle rent the air.

"Beth is sounding the alarm." Julia arched a brow at the dog. "You better go home or you'll be in big trouble."

The animal grinned and rolled over, exposing its furry belly for a scratch.

"You are pitiful. You know that, don't you?" Julia reached for the heart-shaped tag dangling from a bright fluorescent-pink collar. "Belle. They named you Belle? As in beautiful?"

The bushy tail thumped an affirmative.

Julia gave in and rubbed her knuckles against the furry muzzle. The dog's tongue swiped her hand in appreciation.

"Okay, enough of that." Julia chuckled and rose to her feet. The muscles in her thigh contracted in protest. She stared across the field, absently kneading the familiar ache that bloomed in one hip. She looked down at the dog and sighed.

"If I want you to go home, it looks like I'm going to have to take you there myself."

————

"I FOUND BELLE, Dad! She's with Julia."

"Ms. Windham," Cam corrected Beth while inwardly stifling a groan. It was just his luck the dog had decided to trot over and introduce herself to their new neighbor.

He hadn't planned to adopt an animal the same day they moved in, but a logging crew had found Belle running loose in the woods the day before, miles away from any homes or cabins. The closest animal shelter was an hour away, so Tom Blake had agreed to take her in temporarily. Cam had a hunch his new business partner had known that once a certain pint-sized member of the Delaney family met the dog, it would have a permanent home.

His thoughtful boss had even thrown in a brand-new collar and a bag of dog chow.

Cam hadn't minded. One of the reasons he'd looked for a house in the country was so Beth could indulge her love for animals. Something their city apartment lease hadn't allowed.

He could only imagine what Julia would have to say about the first addition to his daughter's menagerie. On second thought, it looked as if he were going to find out. Whether he wanted to or not.

"I'll be there in a minute, sweetheart. Mrs. Robertson and I are almost finished here."

"I believe we are finished." In a sudden flurry of movement, Lucy Robertson began to collect the paperwork. "Call *me*—" Cam didn't miss the slight emphasis on the word "—if you have any questions."

Cam nodded, a little confused by the mixed signals he'd been getting from her. They'd started when he dropped by the realty agency and a subdued Irma Robertson had immediately summoned Lucy instead of dealing with his questions herself. The owner had seemed relaxed and friendly at the office but her attitude had changed the moment she'd arrived at the house. Lucy had been alternately fidgeting, tapping her pen against her teeth and sneaking little glances at the clock for the past half hour.

Now she looked ready to bolt.

"I appreciate your taking the time to make a house call so I could be here to supervise the movers, Mrs. Robertson." Cam smiled. "And please tell Irma that I appreciate her willingness to show me the property last week on such short notice. I still can't believe the way everything worked out."

"Neither can I," Lucy muttered.

"Beth and I can't thank you enough for making this happen."

"Oh, please. Don't thank me." Lucy glanced out the

window and her eyes widened. She began to inch her way toward the door.

"You'll call the Kramers' attorney when you get back to the office? To make sure everything is official?" Everything had happened so fast; Cam didn't want to take any chances. Not when Beth had already claimed the upstairs bedroom as her own.

Lucy's fingers closed around the handle of the screen door. "Of course, but I don't foresee a problem. Your bank called and everything appears to be in order. A second offer should no longer be an issue."

"Second offer?" Cam repeated. "Are you telling me that someone else put in an offer on the house?"

He half expected Lucy to deny it but she hesitated instead. "It's not unusual, you know." The unhappy look on her face told Cam that she regretted mentioning it. "If another buyer comes in and offers cash or has no contingencies, the seller can accept another offer. . ."

And bump the other one out.

Cam exhaled slowly.

The deal had been at risk and he hadn't even been aware of it. While he and Beth had spent the week making plans for their new home, someone had tried to take it away.

Thanks for looking out for us, God.

Cam scraped a hand across his jaw. "I hope the person interested in buying the property won't hold a grudge. I do have to make a living in this town, you know." He was only half joking.

Lucy didn't answer.

Not a good sign.

They heard voices outside and the Realtor paled. "I really should be getting back—"

The bottom dropped out of Cam's stomach as Lucy's peculiar behavior suddenly made sense.

"Julia Windham put the offer in, didn't she?"

Lucy made a strangled sound and her chin jerked once in affirmation.

"But she already has a. . ." Cam stopped himself from saying the word *mansion*. "House. Why does she need another one?"

"It's not a question of need," Lucy explained in a low voice. "When Julia's grandfather was a young man, he deeded some land to his friend Zach Kramer as a gift. Julia isn't interested in the house. This little piece of land. . .your land. . .was part of Wind River Farm once. The Windhams have wanted to buy it back for years."

"So why didn't they buy it after Zach passed away?"

"Because he left it to his older brother—who everyone assumed would sell the place because he lives in California," Lucy explained, obviously warming to the subject even though her voice didn't break above a whisper. "For some reason, Bob Kramer refused. At first it might have been for sentimental reasons but later I think it was out of sheer stubbornness. From what I heard, Tara Windham, Julia's mother, had her attorney pestering him constantly."

"But it was Julia who put in the second offer.

Hoping I'd have a contingency so she could bump me out." Unexpected disappointment crashed over Cam as the truth sank in.

He hadn't expected to join their new neighbor for evening sing-alongs by the campfire but he hadn't expected to get stabbed in the back, either.

Julia hadn't wasted any time trying to get her hands on the property. At least it explained the chilly reception he and Beth had received when they'd shown up on her doorstep.

Cam had been a little disturbed by how often he'd found himself thinking about Julia over the past week. He'd even convinced himself that she was shy rather than standoffish. Reserved rather than snobby.

Now he wondered if Julia had been eating one of the brownies Beth had made while she called the Realtor and tried to take their house away.

To his surprise, Lucy Robertson defended Julia. "If I had to guess, I'd say that Tara probably pressured Julia to put in the offer."

"I didn't meet anyone named Tara. Irma told me that Julia lived alone." That was why Cam had assumed she was a senior citizen.

You assumed a lot, didn't you, buddy?

"She does. Tara moved away shortly after the accident." Lucy's eyes clouded. "Such a tragedy. I'm afraid it changed her. People talked about it for months."

Cam frowned. "Julia's mother was in an accident?"

"No, not Tara. Julia."

27

4

"Isn't Belle sweet, Ms. Windham?"

Julia winced as one of the dog's massive front paws crushed her toes.

Sweet? Not exactly the word *she* would have chosen.

"She's very. . .big."

Beth grinned. "Dr. Blake says she'll be a great watchdog."

Julia hid a smile of her own. She didn't doubt for an instant that the amiable giant would watch a burglar break into the house and help himself to the valuables inside.

"Dad's talking to Mrs. Robertson, and the movers are almost done. Do you want to see my room?"

Now that Julia had successfully reunited the dog with its owner, all she wanted to do was go home. And avoid seeing Cam Delaney again.

She still remembered seeing the confusion—

followed by the flare of panic—in his eyes when she'd hesitated a split second too long before accepting Beth's gift. And if Cam had had an opportunity to talk to Lucy, he would understand the reason *behind* that hesitation. . .

"I don't think—"

"Great. Come on." Beth grabbed her hand and towed her across the muddy yard toward the back door.

Before Julia knew it, she was standing in the kitchen. Face-to-face with the very man she'd wanted to avoid. The abrupt silence that filled the room and the guilty look on Lucy's face told Julia exactly what the topic of their conversation had been.

Something she should have been used to by now.

"Yes, well. . .good luck settling in, Cam. Um, nice to see you again, Julia." The Realtor made a break for it and the screen door snapped shut behind her.

Julia forced herself to meet Cam's gaze and her heart missed a beat.

Over the past week, she'd tried to convince herself that her memory had exaggerated how good looking he was. It hadn't. And that his eyes weren't really *that* green. They were. But when those eyes locked with hers over Beth's head, wariness replaced the friendly warmth Julia had seen in them the day they'd met.

What did you expect, she chided herself. That Cam Delaney would be thrilled when he found out you wanted to take away his house?

• • •

BETH SKIPPED through the maze of cardboard boxes to her father's side. "Julia—I mean Ms. Windham—wants to see my room, Dad," she said cheerfully. "Is that okay?"

One of Cam's dark eyebrows shot up.

Julia's cheeks heated as she choked out a denial. "I didn't say that I. . ." She took a step backward and bumped into a furry wall. A rough, pink tongue swiped her hand.

Beth giggled. "See? Belle likes you."

Julia forced a smile as the dog collapsed at her feet.

Cam's lips twitched. "Thank you for bringing Belle home. She must have escaped when the movers left the door propped open."

Escape sounded good to Julia. Unfortunately, it wasn't an option with a furry chin propped on her shoe.

Beth darted back and tucked her arm through Julia's as if they'd known each other for years. Julia stiffened, not completely comfortable having her personal space invaded so easily. But something about Beth Delaney's sweet personality made it difficult to keep her usual boundaries in place.

"After you see my room, I'll show you the paint that Dad and I picked out," Beth said. "It's called rose petals. Pink is my favorite, favorite—"

"Beth," Cam interrupted, his husky voice pleasant but firm. "We still have a lot of unpacking and I'm sure Ms. Windham has things to do, too. Maybe another time would be better."

He was offering her an out. One Julia should have been eager to accept. . .until she saw the disappointment on Beth's face.

"I suppose I have a minute."

———

Twenty minutes.

Cam paused at the bottom of the staircase. Judging from the trapped look in Julia's eyes, he'd expected her to take a quick peek at Beth's bedroom and then hightail it back home.

Especially after the enlightening conversation he'd had with Lucy Robertson.

Cam shook his head, amazed at the way things had worked out. If even the smallest detail hadn't fallen into place, Julia would own the property and he and Beth would still be searching for a place to live. If Irma Robertson had told him about Julia's interest in the house, he would have backed off and looked for something else. But things hadn't happened that way and Cam recognized a gift when he was given one.

I see your hand in this situation, Lord, but I sure don't know what you've got planned. All I know is that Beth loves this place. . .

And he didn't want that to change.

Cam's fingers closed around the banister as a disturbing thought pushed its way in. If Julia wanted the property so badly, would she happen to mention to

Beth that it had once been part of Wind River Farm? That she'd always intended to buy it back if it came on the market?

Knowing his tenderhearted daughter, her joy would deflate like a day-old helium balloon if she thought they had taken something away—even accidentally—from someone else.

A cardboard box plastered with daisy stickers provided the perfect excuse to find out what was going on. Cam took the stairs two at a time and, as he reached the small landing at the top, he heard the sound of muffled voices coming from Beth's room.

"This one is Gold Dust but I can't remember what kind of horse he is. It's kind of a weird name."

"A Norwegian Fjord," he heard Julia say. "You can tell by the short, two-toned mane."

Cam peeked through the gap in the door and almost dropped the box in his hands.

He'd put the bed frame together shortly after the movers had deposited it in Beth's room but planned to unpack the sheets and blankets later that day when he had more time.

Julia had beaten him to it.

He watched in disbelief as their new neighbor plumped up the pillows and smoothed out the wrinkles in Beth's favorite comforter. His daughter sat perched on a bright pink director's chair near the window, where the dusty ledge provided a temporary corral for her collection of model horses until Cam could put up some shelves.

Beth picked up another horse. "Granna Claire gave me this one for Christmas last year. She's on her honeymoon cruise right now but she promised to bring back a special one for my collection."

"Your *grandmother* is on a honeymoon cruise?"

"Yup. I was her maid of honor," Beth said matter-of-factly, as if there wasn't anything unusual about a grandmother going on a honeymoon cruise. Her voice lowered to a conspiratorial whisper. "Dad and I were the ones who got her and Grandpa Robert together."

"Really?" A soft, musical laugh followed the question.

Cam's heart reacted to the sound by trying to put a hole through his chest. And Cam reacted to that by almost dropping the box. Again.

"Yeah, but I miss her a lot. They won't be able to visit us for a while but Dad promised we can send pictures of the house to them before I go to bed tonight. Granna is going to love it." Beth sounded absolutely certain. "We prayed that Dad and I would find the perfect house, and this is the one God gave us."

Cam closed his eyes briefly, uncertain how Julia would respond to that. His daughter may have been only ten years old but her simple, unwavering faith both humbled and amazed him. Along with her complete unselfconsciousness when it came to sharing it with others!

Through the gap in the door, Cam tried to see Julia's expression but her gaze remained riveted on the faded carpet, the silky tendrils of her tawny hair concealing her profile. But there was no mistaking the rigid set of her shoulders.

"Your dad is probably wondering what's taking us so long," Julia said quietly.

"Can't you stay a little longer?"

The plaintive question raised a warning flag in Cam's mind. Even though Beth was excited about the move, he knew she missed the girl talk that she and her grandmother had frequently indulged in. Something that he felt woefully ill-equipped to duplicate.

Cam was sure that Julia wouldn't be interested in serving as his mother's replacement. But in spite of that certainty, he couldn't help but be intrigued by the subtle contradictions he saw.

When Julia had brought Belle home, he'd braced himself for a lecture about unruly dogs and respecting property lines. Instead, she'd stunned him by giving in to Beth's plea to see her room and then listening patiently to the lengthy introduction—including names *and* breeds—of a herd of model horses.

A tragedy. . .it changed her. Not Julia's mother. . .Julia.

Fragments of his conversation with Lucy Robertson returned. She had mentioned something about Julia being in an accident but hadn't had a chance to elaborate.

But what kind of accident? There were no physical

scars that he could see, but he knew from experience that some of the deepest wounds were on the inside. They were the easiest to conceal and yet they could be just as permanent. And damaging.

Cam couldn't shake the feeling there was more to Julia Windham than met the eye.

"I really do have to go," Julia said. "But thank you for showing me your room. And your horse collection."

Beth's face brightened. "Maybe Belle and I could visit you tomorrow after church."

"I—"

Cam decided it was time to step in. Fast. He cleared his throat to warn them of his approach and then waited a second before shouldering the door open the rest of the way.

"Special delivery for a Bethany Claire Delaney."

"Look, Dad! Julia found all my blankets and made up the bed." Beth flopped across the mattress, hugging a daisy-shaped pillow to her chest.

"I see that. Thank you." Cam watched the color rise in Julia's cheeks before she averted her gaze.

"I prefer to keep busy," she murmured.

Why didn't he believe her? And why did she look embarrassed that he'd caught her doing something nice for Beth?

"Well, I appreciate—" *It.* Cam didn't get a chance to finish the sentence because Julia brushed past him and the faint scent of jasmine stirred the air, temporarily paralyzing his vocal cords.

Beth bounded after Julia, and Cam caught up with them at the bottom of the stairs to run interference. If he wasn't mistaken, Julia was about to be on the receiving end of another hug.

He tried to deflect it. "There's a surprise for you in the living room, Tig."

"Really? What is it?" Beth's excitement over the news spared him a scolding reminder that he wasn't supposed to call her by her nickname anymore.

"See for yourself."

Cam breathed a sigh of relief as Beth veered toward the living room, where he had spread out a checkered blanket in front of the fireplace.

"A picnic!" Beth dropped to her knees and admired the centerpiece—a Mason jar filled with wild violets— that Cam had discovered growing along the foundation of the house. "This is so cool, Dad. What did you make?"

"A call to a local pizza place," Cam admitted. "I haven't unpacked the kitchen boxes yet."

Beth's smile widened to include Julia. "We're having a. . . what's it called again, Dad?"

Cam raked his fingers through his hair. Maybe it hadn't been such a good idea to surprise Beth with a picnic until *after* Julia had left.

"A housewarming party," he muttered.

"That's right. People have one of those when they buy a new house," Beth explained, as if Julia might not be familiar with the tradition. "Only it isn't going to seem like a party with only two people."

Cam didn't need a GPS to follow his pint-size extrovert's train of thought.

"Do you want to celebrate with us?" The question was meant for Julia, but she looked at him to rally support for the idea. "Julia can stay, can't she, Dad? There will be enough pizza—"

A succession of cheerful blasts from a car horn drowned out the rest of the words. Distracted from her closing argument, Beth raced to the window.

"It's Mrs. Robertson!"

Cam strode across the room. Sure enough. Irma Robertson hopped out of a bright yellow van with the words *Lakeshore Community Fellowship* printed on the side.

The doors popped open and people of all ages began to spill out.

"Wow." Beth blinked.

Cam thought that just about summed it up.

Out of the corner of his eye, he saw Julia pivot sharply and walk toward the door.

Beth spotted her, too, and her face fell. "Aren't you going to stay?"

Cam thought he saw a flicker of regret in Julia's eyes, but when their eyes met over Beth's head, the cool mask was back in place. "It looks like you'll have more than enough people to help you celebrate your new house."

5

"Julia knows a lot about horses, Dad."

"Really." Cam kept his tone neutral as he flipped back the blankets on Beth's bed.

"She knows what a Norwegian Fjord is. Isn't that awesome?"

Beth held up one of the model horses, just in case there might come a day when her father would have to identify a Norwegian Fjord, too.

Cam held back a sigh. Julia's name had come up frequently over the course of the day. Too frequently. For a woman who visibly stiffened whenever anyone got within three feet of her, their neighbor had made quite an impression on Beth.

That concerned him.

Jackson Lake was a small town. Julia Windham most likely knew the people that Irma had brought with her the day before and yet she'd disappeared out the back door without saying hello to anyone. Nor had she offered to join the volunteer crew that had given up a Saturday to help him and Beth get settled in.

That told Cam more than anything how Julia felt about them moving next door.

"Into bed now. You've got a big day tomorrow." Cam did the same thing he'd done every time Beth brought up Julia's name. He changed the subject. "Are you sure you don't want me to drive you to school in the morning?"

"I want to ride the bus." Beth wiggled underneath the comforter. "Didn't Julia do a great job making my bed?"

Lord, give me strength.

"I suppose."

"I wonder where she was when Belle and I went to visit her this afternoon."

"When you did what?" Cam choked out the question.

"Went to visit her. I told Julia we'd come over after church today and say hello." Beth's forehead pleated. "But she didn't answer the door when I knocked. Her car was there but maybe she didn't hear me."

Cam closed his eyes. His original plan—*not talking about Julia*—didn't seem to be working.

Why should it? a pesky voice in his head taunted. Not thinking about her doesn't seem to be working, either.

39

Cam pushed the thought away. This was about Beth, not him. And he didn't want his daughter's feelings to be hurt if Julia rebuffed her continued attempts to be friendly.

"Beth—"

"I think I know why God gave us this house, Dad." Beth's winsome smile surfaced and Cam couldn't help but smile back. Not only because it never failed to melt his heart but also because he welcomed the momentary reprieve.

"Why?" He tweaked one of her copper curls. "So you can finally have real animals instead of plastic ones?"

"Nope. For Julia."

"For *Julia?*"

"She's lonely."

"Lone—" The second syllable got stuck in Cam's throat. He tried again. "I don't think she's lonely, sweetheart."

"But she lives all by herself. She doesn't even have a dog."

That's because she didn't want one, Cam was tempted to point out.

"Some people prefer to be alone. And we have to respect their feelings."

"Okay." Beth closed her eyes.

Okay?

"You understand what I'm saying, right?" he pressed. "Julia could be the type of person who likes her privacy. That's the reason she lives in the country. Alone. Without a dog."

"I understand." Beth rolled over. "G'night, Dad. Love you."

Cam stared down at his daughter suspiciously.

Beth understood him. . .but did she *believe* him?

———

"WELL?"

The imperious tone on the other end of the line made Julia wish she had checked her caller ID before answering the phone. Not that she would have ignored a call from her mother but at least she would have had a few seconds to prepare for it.

"Well, what?" Nice try, Julia, but you're only delaying the inevitable.

Her mother's impatient sigh sounded like a tire losing air. "Honestly, Julia, don't pretend you don't know what I'm talking about. Why do you think I called?"

I don't know, Mom. To have a real conversation instead of the usual five-minute duty call you make so you can tell your friends that we talk once a week?

Julia took a restless lap around the room and ended up in front of the window—the one that offered a sweeping view of her property and the house across the pasture—just in time to see a yellow school bus chugging down the road.

As the vehicle rumbled to a stop near the mailbox, Beth streaked out of the house with Belle close behind, playfully nipping at the pink backpack that bumped against her owner's heels.

Beth's first day at her new school.

Judging from the spring in her step, it didn't look as if she was nervous or scared but it couldn't be easy to switch schools at the end of a semester. Julia found herself hoping that Beth would make some friends right away. She remembered what it had felt like to be the "odd man out" on the playground.

Another familiar figure emerged from the house, causing Julia's breath to stick in her throat. It was Monday morning, but Cam, in faded jeans and a sweatshirt, didn't look as if he were dressed to go to the office.

Beth spun around before she clambered up the bus steps and it looked as if she paused to blow her father a kiss.

After the bus rolled around the corner, Cam remained in the driveway, staring at the empty road. Belle sat at his feet and let out a series of sharp little yips, as if demanding to know why her favorite person had disappeared.

Julia felt a tug on her heart. Because something in Cam's posture made her wonder if he wasn't thinking the same thing.

It's just me and Dad.

Beth's words scrolled through her memory. She'd

talked with open affection about her Granna Claire but hadn't mentioned a mother....

"Julia! Are you still there?"

Julia cringed. "Yes, Mom. Still here."

"Then why didn't you answer my question?"

Because I wasn't listening?

Not that Julia was brave enough to admit it. "I'm sorry. I got distracted. I'm in my office."

Staring at my new neighbor.

She wasn't about to admit that, either.

"I asked if you'd offered to give Cam Delaney more than he paid for the place," Tara snapped. "He could find a nice house in Jackson Lake. One that isn't about to fall down around his ears."

Julia thought that was a bit of an exaggeration. True, the outside needed a makeover, but the interior wasn't as bad as she'd imagined it would be. Nothing that some paint and new carpeting wouldn't cure.

"I don't think Cam is interested in selling." Julia watched him pick up a stick and throw it for Belle. He moved with the fluid grace of a natural athlete and she felt a strange flutter in her stomach.

"You don't think Cam is interested in selling," her mother repeated after a moment. "I can't believe you're giving up so easily. I'm disappointed in you, Julia."

Julia felt the sting of the words even though she wasn't surprised by them. After all, she'd been disappointing her mother for years.

We prayed that Dad and I would find the perfect house, and this is the one God gave us.

Unbidden, Beth's words came back to her.

The little girl might believe the house was an answer to prayer, but to Julia it represented one more thing God had taken away from her.

Considering what she'd done, that didn't surprise her, either.

6

Not again.

Cam walked around the house and whistled for Belle, although he had a sinking feeling he knew exactly to where the dog had run off.

The same place she'd run off to three times that morning.

He cupped a hand over his brow to block out the sun and squinted in the direction of Julia's house. Just as he'd suspected, a large white object lay sprawled in front of the door like a furry welcome mat.

Except Cam was pretty certain the welcome didn't extend to the neighbor's dog. Ruefully, Cam admitted that it probably didn't extend to the neighbor, either.

He didn't want to tie up Belle or confine her to the house on a beautiful spring day, but keeping an eye on her was proving to be a challenge while he tackled some of the items on his lengthy to-do list.

Irma Robertson and the volunteers from her congregation had made a significant dent in that list but Cam was still glad he'd put off his official starting date at the vet clinic for a few days. It gave him a chance to start fixing up his fixer-upper.

He started out in the direction of Julia's house, praying she wouldn't step outside and catch Belle trespassing. Or him. So far, he'd managed to pull off three covert ops but the odds of completing another successful mission were getting slim.

He slipped under the fence and sidled along a hedge of arborvitae. When Belle was in sight, he cleared his throat to get the dog's attention. "Come on, girl. This isn't your house."

A carpet-square-size ear twitched, as if a pesky mosquito were buzzing around it.

Cam ran out of hedge and dove behind the nearest lilac bush. "I've got a nice, tasty biscuit on the counter with your name on it."

Belle's eyelids flickered.

Yes. The magic word.

"That's right. Biscuit," Cam whispered.

Wide awake now, the dog lifted her head and let out a happy woof.

Cam shot out from his hiding place. "No! No barking if you want a biscuit—"

So maybe the word wasn't magic. Because Belle rolled to her feet and tipped her nose to the sky. And Cam knew exactly what would happen next.

Aahroorooroo!

He stumbled up the steps and made a grab for the pink collar. And somehow ended up on his back. With Belle on top of him.

"We've got to get home," he gasped, twisting to avoid the swipe of a tongue against his cheek.

Belle didn't budge, leaving Cam to conclude that she had a limited vocabulary. One that included the word *biscuit* but not the word *home.*

"Off you go. Before—"

Julia appeared.

But there she was, staring down at him as if he were a smear on a microscope slide. She somehow managed to look beautiful even upside down; prim and proper in cream-colored chinos and a lightweight yellow sweater that reminded Cam of sunshine.

"Julia." Her name came out in a wheeze.

"Cam." Julia's smile came and went so quickly that Cam decided he must have imagined it. More than likely, the weight on his chest was cutting off oxygen to his brain.

Forget about it, Delaney. You aren't going to get out of this one with your dignity intact.

He tried anyway. "Nice—" *breathe* "—day isn't, it?"

Julia tilted her head and a lock of golden hair followed the movement, caressing the soft curve of her jaw. She clapped her hands twice—she didn't even have to *say* anything—and suddenly he was a free man.

"Thanks." Cam's fingers performed a brief,

exploratory search for broken ribs as he staggered to his feet.

"You're welcome."

They stared at each other.

As if Belle had decided it was her responsibility to break the awkward silence that fell between the humans, she butted her massive head against Julia's leg. Julia caught her lower lip between her teeth and backed away.

Apparently both people *and* dogs were expected to keep their distance.

"Come on, Belle. Time to go home." No way was Cam going to say the word *biscuit* again.

Belle's gaze bounced between him and Julia. And then the dog—*his* dog—sat down. Next to Julia. The plumed tail thumped twice.

Cam interpreted that to mean "so there" in dog-speak.

"Belle. Home."

In response, Belle did a belly flop at Julia's feet, propped her chin on her paws and closed her eyes.

Cam silently added "build kennel" to his to-do list.

"I'm sorry—" He was unable to finish the sentence because he suddenly felt short of breath again. But this time he couldn't blame it on having the canine equivalent of an anvil sitting on his chest.

A smile tipped the corners of Julia's lips. A *real* smile. One that backlit the violet-blue eyes and revealed a captivating dimple in her left cheek.

The unexpected jolt that burned a path from Cam's heart to his toes left him shaken. After eight years, he'd come to accept that *those* kinds of feelings had gone dormant.

There'd been several women in his former congregation who'd subtly let him know they would be open to pursuing a serious relationship but Cam had never been moved by their interest. Now just one smile from Julia Windham left him as tongue-tied as a junior-high kid with his first crush.

Twin spots of color tinted her cheeks.

Oops. Still staring.

Say. Something.

"I guess Belle would rather stay here a little longer." Cam was even more stunned by the realization that he didn't blame the dog a bit. He was tempted to linger, too. Which was crazy, considering the fact that Julia didn't want him on her property. Or living in the house next door.

"Excuse me." Julia ducked her head but not before Cam caught a glimpse of another smile. "I'll let the two of you work this out while I check my mail."

She started down the steps and Belle rolled to her feet, attaching herself to Julia's side like a well-trained service dog.

Building the kennel moved to the top of the list. "We'll, ah, walk with you. We're heading in that direction anyway." Cam tried to focus on something else so she wouldn't catch him staring. Again.

"It's hard to get used to the quiet," he said, lifting his face to the sun as they fell in step together down the driveway.

"Quiet?"

Cam chuckled at the astonishment in Julia's voice. Okay, the birds' lively chorus in the trees around them didn't exactly meet the definition. "It's hard to get used to the sounds of nature instead of sirens and traffic."

"Not everyone adjusts to country living."

"You did."

Julia's gaze remained fixed ahead of them. "Sometimes a person doesn't have a choice. Sometimes they have to. . .adjust. Whether they want to or not."

There was something in her voice that Cam couldn't quite identify. Resignation? Regret?

"Growing up, I was a frustrated city boy. I must have read *Hatchet* a dozen times and I remember driving my mother crazy every time she found me sleeping under my bed instead of on top of it." Cam smiled at the memory. "Beth takes after me, I suppose. Her mother's idea of roughing it was staying at a hotel without a concierge."

If Cam were honest with himself, it was one of the reasons he'd stayed in the city so long. Chicago had been the place where he and Laurel had met and eventually married. The place he felt closest to her. Moving away would have felt as if he were severing another connection. So he'd stayed. Until his mother had challenged him to pray about his future, and the answer had ultimately led him to a dilapidated two-story house. A house that already felt like home.

"But. . .Beth's mother will visit here, won't she? She'll want to see Beth's room and meet Belle."

Cam sucked in a breath, reminding himself that Julia wouldn't know anything about his personal life.

"Laurel—" it didn't hurt quite as much when he said her name anymore "—died when Beth was two years old."

Julia's mask slipped and her eyes filled with compassion. "I'm so sorry. I assumed. . ."

"That I was divorced," Cam finished. "Don't worry. It's an honest mistake. Not too many guys are widowers at the age of twenty-four."

He still couldn't believe eight years had gone by. Sometimes it seemed as if the accident had happened a few days ago. At other times, it felt like a lifetime ago.

"Laurel had met some friends for lunch and was on her way home. A driver ran a red light at the intersection." A condensed version of a day that had come close to destroying the underpinnings of Cam's life. And faith.

If Laurel hadn't left Beth at his mother's, he might have lost them both.

"I'm sorry."

Cam had heard those formal little words spoken dozens of times from people who had inadvertently stumbled into a similar conversation. But the faint tremor in Julia's voice went beyond sympathy. It sounded like. . .understanding.

She'd lost someone, too.

Who?

As much as Cam wanted to know the answer to that question, he wasn't about to risk the fragile connection that had sprung up between them.

Lost in thought, he suddenly realized that Julia had stopped at the end of the driveway. Two mailboxes were fastened to a single post. One of them was scratched and dented. The door sagged open on its hinges, an open invitation to whatever forest creature had obviously taken shelter there over the winter.

"I don't have to ask which mailbox belongs to you and which one is mine." Cam couldn't prevent the low rumble of laughter that escaped. "It looks like I'll have to add 'put up a new mailbox' to my list."

"After you paint Beth's room?"

Cam frowned. "How did you know I was painting her room?"

"You have, um, pink paint. On your cheek."

Of course he did. Because being turned into a throw rug by a Samoyed-shepherd mix hadn't been humiliating enough.

Cam performed an exploratory search along his jaw. "Did I get it?"

"No, it's right. . .here." At the feather-light touch of Julia's fingers against the side of his face, Cam felt another breaker switch in his heart flip on.

Julia yanked her hand away and her eyes darkened with confusion.

That makes two of us, Cam thought.

He forced a rueful smile, sensing that Julia was ready to bolt. "Beth's favorite, favorite color."

"Rose petals."

Cam was surprised she'd remembered. "I guess it's a good thing she didn't insist on painting the outside of the house that color."

"You're painting the house?"

"Weren't you going to?" Cam asked without thinking.

A pause. And then, "I was going to have it taken down."

"Taken. . ." Cam's voice trailed off when the meaning sank in. "As in, demolished?"

"That's right." Julia's gaze shifted to the house. *His* house. "It's old and falling apart. It's an eyesore."

Why did he get the feeling she was repeating someone else's words?

"I guess that depends on whose eyes are looking at it," Cam said softly.

Julia didn't reply as she pulled a stack of envelopes out of her mailbox.

"I'm sorry about Belle," he said, reluctant to leave things between them on a bad note. "Beth and I will work on training her to stay in the yard."

Julia's hand kneaded the soft curve of her hip. "Thank you," she said, her tone once again polite.

Distant. "I work out of my home so my hours vary every day. It's difficult to get anything accomplished if there are constant distraction."

Cam read between the lines. Distractions like a precocious ten-year-old and her ninety-pound canine sidekick.

He tamped down the disappointment that stirred inside of him. With a little creativity, Cam knew he could keep the ninety-pound sidekick out of Julia's hair —and her yard. But he had a feeling a precocious ten-year-old would prove to be the greater challenge.

J ulia's cell phone came to life in her jacket pocket, belting out the theme song from one of her favorite musicals.

"Hello?"

"Julia?"

At the sound of Cam's voice, the wooden spoon she'd been using to stir a batch of homemade spaghetti sauce slipped out of her hand and clattered across the kitchen floor.

"I'm sorry. Did I catch you in the middle of something?"

Just thinking about you was the first thought that popped into Julia's head.

"N-no." Her hands trembled as she bent to retrieve the spoon.

"I hate to bother you." Cam's ragged exhale on the

other end of the line had Julia's fingers tightening around the phone.

"Is everything all right? Is it Beth?" The questions tumbled over each other.

"She's the reason I'm calling," Cam admitted. "I'm on my way to a house call. A dog was struck by a car and its owner is an elderly woman who lives alone. I usually pick Beth up after school and she stays at the clinic with me until we close for the day."

Julia connected the dots.

He needed her help.

"What about Irma Robertson? Or Lucy?" she blurted.

"Oh." There was a pause and Julia's could almost *see* Cam run his fingers through his hair. It was a little unsettling to discover that she was already familiar with some of his mannerisms. "I thought of you first."

Strangely enough, a feeling of warmth, rather than panic, bloomed inside of her at the admission.

"Beth needs a ride home from school?"

"No, I called the principal and Beth can take the bus home today. It's just that I'm not comfortable with her being alone, especially when I don't know how long this will take. I should have asked Irma. You're probably busy."

Not to mention she'd more or less told Cam that she preferred to be left alone. They both knew it— although he was too polite to remind her of their last conversation. The conversation that had plagued her with guilt—and regret—ever since.

It had been an evasive maneuver. A futile attempt to override the urge to comfort him when he'd told her that his wife had died. To tell him that she understood grief. And loss.

The troubling part was that even though she hadn't said a word, Cam had still known. She'd heard it in his voice. Seen it in his eyes. The fact that he'd looked past her defenses and discovered the truth had stirred up her flight response.

When she'd told Cam that she didn't need any unnecessary distractions, he'd thought she meant Beth and the dog. But the truth was, she found Cam a distraction, too. His appealing, lopsided smile. The husky, masculine laugh that wove its way through the frozen terrain of her heart, melting a path through her defenses like a warm spring breeze.

If she weren't careful, it would be all too easy to let Cam and Beth Delaney into her life. In less than a week, they already occupied more of her thoughts than they should. Beth's sweet personality and impulsive hugs made Julia long for things she could never have. And Cam. . .

She refused to let her thoughts go there.

Julia tried to come up with an excuse. A valid reason why having Beth over wouldn't work out. But she couldn't think of a single one.

"I'm not busy," she heard herself say instead. "Beth can stay here until you get home."

Silence. And then, "Great. I'll be there as soon as I can." The relief in his voice was palpable.

"Don't worry. She'll be fine."

"Oh, I'm not worried about Beth." Cam chuckled. "I know she'll be in good hands. I'm just sorry I had to inconvenience you."

"It's not an inconvenience." As soon as she said the words, Julia realized they were true. She didn't know what Cam had said to Beth, but neither the little girl nor her dog had made any impromptu visits over the past few days. Even though she tried to convince herself it was what she'd wanted, she couldn't help but feel a little. . .disappointed.

"Great. I'll see you soon."

Julia hung up the phone and glanced at the clock. In half an hour, Beth would be getting off the bus.

Panic squeezed the air from her lungs.

Was she supposed to fix her an after-school snack? Did she have anything in the cupboard that would appeal to a ten-year-old? Should she help with homework?

I know she'll be in good hands.

Cam's words scrolled through her mind, easing her momentary panic. He'd sounded so confident.

Why did he trust her?

She'd been less than neighborly since they'd moved in next door. Rebuffed Beth's invitation to share a picnic lunch. She'd even put in a generous offer on the house that Beth believed God had provided for them.

Julia had tried to keep a safe distance but the feelings that Cam stirred inside of her felt anything but safe. Watching him and Beth interact—seeing the affection between them—made her long for things beyond her reach. Things she'd accepted would never be part of her life. A close, loving family. A home filled with laughter.

In a single moment, those dreams had shattered along with the bones in her body. For a little while, her fiancé had held her hand and made her believe that everything would be all right. But in the end, Steve had walked away, too.

There was no point in dreaming. Not when dreams only led to disappointment.

————

QUARTER TO NINE.

Cam winced, mentally practicing the apology he owed Julia.

He'd kept his promise—to get home as soon as he could. The trouble was, this was the soonest he could get home. Which meant Julia had been in charge of homework, supper and the general all-around mayhem that typically accompanied Beth's bedtime routine.

Maybe he should have stopped at the grocery store

and bought a box of chocolates to go along with the apology.

Or maybe you shouldn't have called her in the first place.

Why had he? A split second after Julia had answered the phone, Cam had wondered why she'd been the first person who had come to mind when he'd been called out on an emergency. After stumbling through the explanation as to *why* he'd called, he half expected she would laugh. Or hang up on him.

He'd almost dropped the phone when she'd agreed to keep an eye on Beth until he could get home. And he hadn't imagined the undercurrent of concern in her voice when she'd asked if everything was all right. As if she actually *cared* that everything was all right.

But that didn't make sense, either, considering she'd all but told him that she wanted to be left alone.

Over the past few days, Cam had done his best to keep his determined offspring so busy that she didn't have time to slip under the fence and drop by their neighbor's house for a visit.

He'd hinted that Julia worked out of her home. . .*no, he had no idea what she did.* . .and that she wasn't too keen on being disrupted. . .*yes, it was possible Belle fell into that category.* . .so it was important to respect people's wishes. And their privacy.

Beth had accepted everything he'd said but that didn't stop her from talking about Julia. Every chance she got. Or adding Julia's name to the list of people she prayed for at bedtime.

God, thank You that we moved here.

The first time Cam heard that one, it was all he could do to stifle a groan. If Julia talked with God at all, he doubted she was saying a similar prayer.

Still, there were moments when their new neighbor seemed to soften; making him wonder if some lingering pain below the surface had forged the cool reserve she used like a shield.

He thought about the smile she hadn't been able to suppress when Belle had plopped at her feet that day. The smile that continued to linger at the edges of his memory.

You keep lecturing Beth on keeping your distance. You should probably take your own advice, Cam chided himself.

As he guided the car around the corner, his foot came down hard on the brake. Julia's house was completely dark except for a soft glow in the kitchen window. His house, on the other hand, was lit up like a float in the annual Christmas parade.

It occurred to him that they'd probably switched houses because it was getting close to the time Beth went to bed and Julia didn't know when he'd be home.

Because my cell phone battery died. And Mrs. Vander-beek's dog needed emergency surgery. . .

He parked the car and slipped inside the house, half

expecting to find Julia waiting for him on the other side of the door. Tapping her foot.

THE FRONT HALL WAS EMPTY. There was no sign of Belle, who usually greeted him the moment she heard his key turn in the lock. Everything was quiet. So quiet that Cam wondered if he *had* gone to wrong house by mistake.

He made a quick search of the first floor and then padded up the stairs. When he reached the top step, he saw a sliver of light underneath Beth's bedroom door. Cam tapped on it before turning the knob.

"Anybody in here?" He pushed it open, his heart fisting at the sight that greeted him.

His daughter was already in her favorite pajamas and tucked under the covers. Propped up on her knees was the book of family devotions they read together every night.

That part of the scene was familiar one to Cam. The one that stole his breath from his lungs was the fact that she was leaning against Julia, their heads close together. Julia's legs were tucked underneath her, the powder-blue sweater she wore embellished with a necklace made of braided ribbon and gaudy beads.

In spite of the differences in their coloring, she and Beth looked as if they fit together like the last two pieces of a puzzle.

Cam felt the world suddenly shift beneath his feet.

Swamped by an unexpected wave of emotion, he struggled to regain his equilibrium.

For eight years, he'd done everything he could to make sure that Beth didn't feel the void that Laurel's death had created in their family. His mother had provided a wonderful role model. He'd made sure Beth had regular playdates with friends. He encouraged her interests and hobbies.

Cam had convinced himself that his daughter had everything she needed. Their lives were full. Their family complete, even though it was only the two of them.

What he hadn't known until this moment was that he'd tried to convince himself of that, too.

The thought slammed against his defenses. Defenses that Cam hadn't even known existed. Until now.

For years he'd refused to date, telling himself that he needed to protect Beth from the complications a serious relationship would inevitably bring. But now, as if God were aiming a light into a shadowy corner of his soul, it occurred to Cam that maybe, just maybe, Beth's heart hadn't been the only one he'd been protecting.

8

"Are you okay, Dad?"

Something must have shown on his face because Beth's eyes rounded in alarm.

Cam wasn't sure how to answer that particular question so he avoided it by asking one of his own. "How did everything go?"

Beth grinned. "Good. We finished reading today's devotion and we were just about to pray."

Daily devotional readings. Prayer. These things were a benediction at the close of every day in the Delaney household. But what had Julia thought about the unexpected additions to her responsibilities?

Which reminded Cam how late it was.

How late *he* was.

He dared a quick look in Julia's direction. "I'm sorry you had to bring Beth back here for bedtime."

"We never went to my house. We decided it would

be easier to stay here." Nothing in Julia's expression gave Cam a clue how she felt about the change in venue. Or anything else, for that matter.

Beth nodded vigorously. "We took Belle for a walk. And I had to feed the rabbits and put fresh bedding in their hutch."

Cam had forgotten about the rabbits. They'd recently adopted Sam and Walter from Mrs. Carlson, one of Dr. Blake's clients. Apparently, word was getting out that the Delaney family had a soft spot for critters of all kinds.

"Did you finish your homework?"

"I didn't have any tonight." Beth caught the devotional book as it started to slide off her knees.

Cam's vision of Beth spending the evening engrossed in her homework while Julia went about her own business dissolved as swiftly as the apology he'd rehearsed on the way home. "What did you do?" He was almost afraid to ask.

"After supper we made chocolate-chip cookies for your lunch and Julia put up the curtains in my room." Beth's expression brightened. "Oh, we talked to Granna Claire, too."

His mother had called?

Wait a second. Had Beth just said, "*We*"?

"She said she'll call again when they reach the next port," Julia said briskly as she slid off the bed.

Right. If Cam knew his mother, she'd be calling a lot sooner than that.

Julia looked poised for flight but Cam stood between her and the door. "Thank you again for keeping an eye on Beth."

"And Belle and Sam and Walter," his daughter chimed in.

Cam winced. There should have been an apology, chocolate, *and* flowers.

"Thank you for taking care of everyone," he amended.

"We had fun, didn't we, Julia?" Beth gave a contented sigh.

"Yes, we did." The flicker of vulnerability in Julia's eyes tugged at Cam's heart. As if she had surprised herself by admitting it.

"'Night." Beth stifled a yawn. "You can keep the necklace."

Julia glanced at the colorful garland of ribbon that circled her neck. For a split second, the elusive dimple surfaced. "Thank you."

"I'll give you a ride home." Now that Cam thought about it, he hadn't noticed her car parked by the house.

"I don't mind walking." Julia politely but firmly rejected his offer. "I can cut across the pasture."

"It's no. . ." *Trouble.*

Cam found himself talking to empty air.

———

HE CAUGHT up to her at the door.

"I really don't mind walking." Julia refused to look at him. *Couldn't* look at him. "It's a beautiful night."

"You're right about that." Cam's broad shoulders lifted in an easy shrug as he fell in step beside her. "Which is exactly why I don't mind walking you home."

"Beth—"

"Is watching us from the bedroom window. She and Belle will be fine for a few minutes."

Julia was glad the shadows concealed her panic. She didn't want to be anywhere near Cam Delaney. All she wanted to do was put the evening behind her and be alone.

Liar.

She stumbled a little, as if the truth had knocked her off balance. Because she hadn't wanted to go home. She'd wanted to stay.

An evening with Beth had given Julia a bittersweet glimpse of the kind of life she'd stopped dreaming about a long time ago.

They had done all the things Beth had told her father about, and a few more besides. The only awkward moment was when Granna Claire had asked to speak with her. Julia had reluctantly taken the phone from Beth, certain she'd be subjected to an interrogation.

Instead, Cam's mother had expressed her gratitude that Julia had come to his rescue.

"I'm so thankful they have a neighbor like you," Claire had gushed. *"I have to admit I've struggled with guilt over being so far away but it helps to be reminded that God is*

looking out for them. I hope I get a chance to meet you when Robert and I come for a visit."

Julia had squirmed under the praise. If Cam's mother knew what had transpired with the house, she wouldn't be so quick to believe Julia was an answer to her prayers.

She wasn't an answer to anyone's prayers.

Especially someone like Cam. Not only was he incredibly attractive on the outside, Julia was discovering that his insides were just as appealing. He was a devoted family man. A man who opened his home to a growing menagerie of animals. A man who would eventually remarry and fill the house with brothers and sisters for Beth. . .

This time, the pain surging through her had nothing to do with the tiny spasms that shot up her leg as Julia quickened her pace. A futile attempt to outrun her thoughts.

"Hey, slow down." The husky amusement in Cam's voice rubbed against her already raw defenses. "Are you training for a marathon or something?"

Afraid he would see her expression, Julia stopped at the edge of the yard, where the moonlight merged with the shadows. "You don't have to go any farther. Beth will be waiting up for you and it's getting late."

Cam's chiseled features were washed in silver, his jade eyes searching as he stared down at her. For one heart-stopping moment, Julia thought he would insist.

"All right." She breathed a sigh of relief when he

gave in. "Listen, I really do appreciate you putting aside your plans tonight to watch Beth."

Plans?

If the idea hadn't been so laughable, Julia might have smiled. Her plans for the evening had included curling up on the sofa with the book she'd been reading. Nothing that couldn't be put off until the following day. Or the next.

A week ago, if anyone asked, Julia would have insisted she was content with her solitary life. The life she'd chosen. But a few hours in the Delaney household had made that life seem boring. Empty.

There's no place for you there, she reminded herself ruthlessly as she pivoted away from Cam.

"What can I do to thank you?" he called after her. "I grill a great steak. And I've been told I make a mean hot fudge sundae, too."

More time spent in his company. Another evening being reminded of what she couldn't have. So why did a wave of longing rush through her? It took all Julia's will to keep walking, her frayed emotions unraveling with each step she took away from him.

"If you won't tell me, I'll have to come up with something on my own."

Julia knew she should turn around and tell Cam that he didn't owe her anything.

She found herself smiling instead.

And that was what frightened her the most.

9

"**J**ulia helped me make necklaces for all the horses," Beth said between bites of pancake. "And she held Walter and Sam while I cleaned out their cage."

Okay. Cam *really* had to find a way to make it up to her.

The trouble was, every time Beth said Julia's name—and so far, their entire breakfast conversation had revolved around the evening she and Beth had spent together—Cam swore he heard the sound of yet another wall crumbling around his heart.

He'd lain awake half the night, asking God why Julia Windham was the one who'd managed, in the brief time he'd known her, to resurrect feelings he'd thought had died with Laurel.

"More pancakes?" Cam tried to distract Beth from any more talk about their next-door neighbor.

"Nope." Beth swallowed the last of her orange juice. "Julia said—"

"The bus will be here in a few minutes, Tig."

Beth rolled her eyes. "I'll be eleven on Friday, Dad. Remember?"

Cam smiled. How could he forget, when she reminded him at least twice a day? At least he'd hit upon a topic guaranteed to turn Beth's attention away from Julia.

"Have you decided how we should celebrate your birthday?"

"Can Julia come over and have cake with us? You said I could invite some friends over."

Give me patience, Lord. And right now would be great. "I meant friends from school."

"I don't have any friends yet."

"No friends?" Cam raised an eyebrow. Both the principal and Beth's teachers had assured him that she'd adjusted well to her new school and was popular with her classmates.

"Maybe a few." Beth stirred a pool of maple syrup around with her fork. "But it's tough being the new kid." Sorrowful eyes peered up at him.

Cam was tempted to ask if the school had a drama club she could join.

"Julia might have other plans," he said carefully. "Remember what we talked about—"

"Bus is coming!" Beth dove for the pink backpack at her feet. "Gotta go. Love ya, Dad!" She paused when

71

she reached the door and tossed a smile over her shoulder. "By the way, Julia doesn't have a boyfriend. I asked her."

The door snapped shut but Cam's lower jaw was still hanging open.

A few seconds later, his cell rang, jarring him out of the near-catatonic state that Beth's parting words had put him in.

"I was hoping I'd catch you before you left for work."

He knew it. "Hi, Mom. You weren't supposed to call until the weekend. Is everything all right?"

"That's my line." Claire chuckled. "You sound a little dazed."

That about summed it up, Cam thought. "Just trying to figure something—" *someone* "—out."

"Beth."

"Bingo." Cam decided it was best not to mention the other woman in his life he couldn't figure out. Whoa. Wait a second. There *was* no other woman in his life. "I'm not sure what to do with her."

"What's going on?"

"She's getting a little attached to our new neighbor." And there, Cam thought, was a perfect example of the pot calling the kettle black.

"Ah, Julia Windham." Was it his imagination, or did his mother sound a bit smug? "She seems like a very nice young woman. What's the problem?"

So Cam told her. Everything. How Julia had

planned to buy the property. Her assertion that she didn't need distractions and then not hesitating to give up an evening to keep an eye on Beth. About Beth's insistence that Julia was lonely.

When he finished, there was absolute silence on the other end of the line. Cam waited. His mother not only knew her granddaughter well but she practically oozed wisdom. He was confident she could shed some light on the situation.

"Oh."

"Oh?" Cam repeated the word in disbelief. "That's it? That's all you've got?"

"I. . ." Claire hesitated. "I think I might know why Beth is so determined to befriend Julia."

Relief poured through Cam. "Great."

"You might not think so when you hear my theory," she murmured. "Normally, I wouldn't share a confidence, but in this case I should probably make an exception. Beth told you about her special prayer—"

"For the house."

"Yes. That was one of them."

"There's more than one?"

A sigh unfurled on the other end of the line. "You know Beth keeps a list of the things she prays for in her diary. Before Robert and I left on our honeymoon she shared her top three with me. A house in the country was the first one."

Cam waited. And waited. "Mom, I'm a big boy, remember? Let's hear number two."

"A horse."

Cam relaxed a little. So far, no surprises. Beth's love for that particular animal was no secret. "I know all about that one, too."

"Yes, well. . ."

"Come on, Mom. Give it to me straight," Cam teased. "I think I can handle—"

"Beth has been asking God for a mother."

"What?"

"That's not all."

How, Cam wondered in disbelief, could there possibly be more?

"I have a feeling she thinks that God took care of two requests at the same time."

"Two requests?"

"Look at it from her perspective," Claire said, and for the first time Cam heard an undercurrent of amusement in her voice. "God provided the house in the country. And Julia—an attractive, young, and, I might add, conveniently single—woman who happens to live right next door."

———

JULIA RETREATED to the woods right after breakfast to clear her head. And to escape the verse she'd read in Beth's devotional book the night before.

It didn't work. If anything, it seemed as if everything around her kept repeating the words like a chorus.

The breeze that whispered through the hardwoods. The birds singing in the branches above her head.

Trust in the Lord and do good. Dwell in the land and enjoy safe pasture. Delight yourself in the Lord and He will give you the desires of your heart.

Had she ever truly trusted Him?

At one point in her life, she would have said she did.

But then, Julia thought bitterly, she also would have claimed she had everything her heart desired.

As the only child of the wealthiest family in the area, Julia grew up believing that Wind River Farm was the equivalent of a tiny kingdom. And from the moment Julia had been placed on the back of a horse at the age of four, she'd been expected to carry on the legacy that her mother, a former superstar in eventing competitions, had begun.

To a girl whose baby book claimed that one of her first words was "horsey," the hours she'd spent caring for the horses and taking riding lessons had never seemed like a burden. Julia preferred spending time in the barn to hanging out with her classmates, who mistook her shyness for arrogance. Not only that, but the barn offered a refuge when her parents' arguing escalated to the point that her father had walked out the door one day and never come back.

After he left, Tara had pushed her even harder. As trophies began to line the mantel, life became more about the exacting requirements of the ring and less about the simple pleasures Julia had found in a leisurely ride along the river. It hadn't taken long for her to figure out that a judge's approval rating earned approval in her mother's eyes—something she longed for more than another ribbon or trophy.

Julia continued to meet every challenge, and her fearless confidence both in and out of the ring cemented her reputation as the golden girl of the horse show circuit. The reigning princess from Wind River Farm.

And then she'd met her prince.

Julia closed her eyes but it didn't prevent an image of Steve Larsen's handsome face from invading her memories. Their paths had crossed at a weekend cross-country event and he'd asked her to dinner. Three months later, he'd proposed.

She'd had everything. Until the accident.

Julia had returned to Wind River Farm, not at the top of the world but in pieces at the bottom of it. Everything had changed. Tara had accepted a position teaching at a prestigious riding academy in Kentucky and Steve had broken off their engagement.

But a fiancé wasn't all she'd lost.

Julia sank against a tree.

When Beth had read the words in the devotional book the night before, a surge of longing had swept through her. And Julia knew why. She was tired of going through the motions of each day, alive but not really living. To anyone watching, she appeared to have everything together. Only Julia knew the truth. The injuries may have healed but the wounds on her heart hadn't.

Trust in the Lord.

Could she?

Julia closed her eyes and her heart formed the words before her mind could shut them down.

Please tell me that You're here, God. And that You care about me.

When she opened them again, she could see the faint outline of Cam's house beyond the trees.

Cam's house.

A smile curved her lips.

When had she stopped thinking of it as the old Kramer place?

When had she'd stopped thinking of it as *hers*?

Maybe when she'd realized that she loved seeing lights glow in the windows at night. Watching Belle chase squirrels around the yard. Hearing Cam's tuneless whistle when he was outside working. Witnessing the slow transformation that was turning a weary-looking house into a home.

Knowing that Cam and Beth belonged there.

Beth believed the house was an answer to prayer but was it possible it was the answer to hers, too?

10

"**O**kay, God. I'm listening."

Unfortunately, all Cam heard in response was silence. No still, small voice. Only the birds and the excited chatter of a red squirrel warning its forest friends about the intruders who'd crossed into their territory.

After the conversation with his mother, Cam needed to clear his head before he went to work. And since he couldn't hit the gym, he hit the trail along the river instead.

He still had a hard time believing that Beth had been asking God for a mother. But what was even more difficult to believe was that Beth thought Julia was the answer to her prayer! Julia lived in the country but spent most of her time indoors. She wasn't an animal lover. She froze whenever anyone invaded her personal space. . .

Except for last night.

Before he could prevent it, an image of Beth, nestled comfortably against Julia while they read the devotional book, popped up in Cam's mind. Immediately followed by another. The flash of longing he'd seen in Julia's eyes when he'd walked her home. It had taken all his self-control not to pull her into his arms but she'd severed the connection between them by walking away. She'd rejected his awkward invitation to dinner. In fact, other than a few rare smiles, she hadn't given any indication that she was interested in him. In fact, she made it a point to show him just the opposite.

Because she's afraid of what she's feeling. Just like you are.

Now Cam heard the still, small voice.

"I'm not afraid," Cam muttered. "I. . .content."

Content with memories of the brief but happy years of marriage to Laurel, his high-school sweetheart. Content with the career he'd chosen. Content to pour his time and energy into their only child.

Wasn't that a good thing?

Cam couldn't help sounding a wee bit defensive when he'd directed the question at his mother.

"Contentment *is* a good thing. Protecting your heart from pain isn't," Claire had gently pointed out on the phone. "When I was about to turn down Robert's invitation to go out for dinner, a wise person said that I should be open to God's leading, even if it meant leaving my comfort zone."

Cam knew exactly who the wise person was that she'd referred to. But he hadn't expected his mother would turn his words around and use them on him.

The situation was completely different.

He'd have to have a talk with his daughter, that was all there was to it. Just because they'd moved next door to a young, single woman didn't mean that God had handpicked Julia Windham to be Beth's mother.

Or his wife.

He and Julia were neighbors. They'd barely formed a truce, let alone a friendship. Cam couldn't see anything else happening between him and Julia.

Even though you would like it to.

"A guy can only take so much rejection, Lord," Cam muttered. "I'd have to see a major breakthrough in Julia's attitude to even consider. . ." His voice trailed off.

Why was he considering anything?

Cam groaned. This was Beth's fault. And his mother's. For putting thoughts in his head that had no business being there.

Rather than wandering around like Moses in the desert, Cam decided it would be better to go to the office and focus on his work.

Speaking of wander. Cam frowned. He'd lost his walking buddy.

"Belle!" He called the dog's name and tilted his head to listen, expecting any moment to hear her crashing through the underbrush.

Nothing.

With a resigned sigh and a vow to bring a leash next time, Cam started toward the creek. The dog loved to wade in the ice-cold water.

As he worked his way through the brush, he passed one of the many yellow No Trespassing signs that peppered the woods between the two properties.

The irony wasn't lost on him.

"That means you," he reminded himself sternly. "Julia Windham doesn't want anyone trespassing on her property. Or in her life."

Another trail opened up near a clearing by the river and as Cam rounded the corner, he heard Belle begin to bark. The frantic bark reserved for the impudent squirrels that dared to mock her from the safety of a branch above her head.

Cam broke into a jog as Belle continued to raise a ruckus loud enough to be heard in town. Julia had already caught them on her porch. He didn't want her to catch them trespassing on her property, too.

"Belle! Come here, girl." Cam knew he was probably wasting his breath but if the dog stopped barking long enough to look at him, at least his eardrums would have a few precious seconds to recover.

Belle's head turned in his direction and there was a blessed moment of silence. Then she started up again.

Cam vaulted over a fallen log and almost fell flat on his face in his haste to get to the animal. "Do you know what the word *trespassing* means? It means that if Julia finds us here, we're going to be in big trouble."

Belle's frantic barking subsided to a high-pitched whine but she continued to dance around the trunk of the tree.

"When are you going to learn that you can't bark a squirrel out of a tree?" Cam peered up at the branches, expecting to see one of the fuzzy little critters grinning down at them.

What he didn't expect to see was. . .Julia.

He blinked, just to make sure she didn't vanish like some kind of forest sprite. No. Still there. And not looking at all happy to see him. Belle, on the other hand, gave him a smug, see-what-I-found grin.

"You're sitting in a tree." Brilliant powers of observation. Maybe you should have been a detective instead of a veterinarian.

"And you're trespassing."

Cam had hoped she wouldn't notice. But apparently, he wasn't the only one who possessed brilliant powers of observation. "You weren't spying on me, were you?" The thought, however far-fetched, cheered him.

"No." Julia looked a little nonplussed by the suggestion. "Just thinking. *Alone.*"

Instead of taking the hint, Cam leaned against a tree and stuffed his hands in his pockets. "Great. Let me know when you're done."

She gaped at him. "You aren't going to wait for me."

"That's the plan."

"I climbed up here," Julia pointed out. "I can get back down again."

"Convince me."

"I've climbed this tree a hundred times. Look at the branches. It's like going up and down a ladder."

Cam studied the large gaps between the gnarled limbs of the oak. "You're right, I have seen ladders like this. In Beth's Dr. Seuss books."

Something in his expression must have convinced Julia that he wasn't going anywhere. She started climbing down.

By the time she reached the last branch, Cam was there, ready and waiting for that final four-foot drop. His hands closed around Julia's narrow waist as she swung down.

"Feel better?" Julia grumbled the moment her feet touched the ground.

"Yes." A lot better. That was the trouble. It suddenly occurred to Cam that he hadn't let go of her yet. It suddenly occurred to him that he didn't *want* to.

"Cam."

When Julia whispered his name, Cam couldn't have stopped himself from looking at her lips if his life had depended on it. He lowered his head, wondering if they were as sweet as he imagined.

What. Are. You. Thinking.

Out of nowhere, the voice of reason drenched him like a bucket of cold water. Reminded Cam that if he crossed that line, she would never speak to him again.

"I'm sorry—" Cam stopped, fascinated by the blush

of color that stained Julia's cheeks. And the look of absolute disappointment on her face.

She pivoted away from him and started down the trail.

If Cam's knees hadn't turned to sponges, he would have gone after her. He looked down at Belle.

"Do you think that qualifies as a breakthrough in her attitude?"

The dog barked once in affirmation and Cam grinned.

"So do I."

ulia? I was hoping I'd catch you at home."

When was her heart going to stop ricocheting around in her chest whenever she heard Cam Delaney's voice?

Fortunately, it was easier to deal with him on the telephone than in person. On the phone Julia didn't have to shore up her defenses against an engaging smile and a pair of warm green eyes.

"I'm actually not at home right now. I'm at the grocery store."

"I'm afraid this is becoming a habit. Calling you in the middle of the day to ask for a favor." Cam's low laugh proved to be just as dangerous to Julia's peace of mind. It conjured up memories of the day before, when he'd caught her sitting in the tree.

She'd heard Belle barking and Cam whistling for her to come back. She'd hoped neither of them would find her. She hadn't anticipated the dog could boast a bit of bloodhound in its genes. Upon discovery, Julia had done her best to brazen her way through it and she'd nearly succeeded. . .

Until Cam had almost kissed her.

It was your imagination, she told the mischievous voice in her head.

Mmm. So you must have imagined your disappointment, too?

This time, she ignored the pesky thought.

Cam had escorted her to the property line, but once they'd gone their separate ways all of Julia's old fears had crowded in. She wanted to believe. To trust. But what would happen if she lost everything again?

"What can I do for you?" She was relieved to discover that her voice was steadier than her shaking hands.

"I don't know if Beth mentioned that her birthday is today?"

"A few times." Julia smiled. More like half a dozen. "She seemed pretty excited even though she got her gift early."

"Early?"

"Belle. I remember Beth saying that she was hoping to get a puppy this year."

"Yes, well. . .I found something else. Irma Robertson is taking Beth out for ice cream after school and I was wondering if I could stash the present in your barn. To surprise her when she gets home."

"I suppose so." Julia fought to keep her emotions grounded against the ridiculous surge of pleasure at being included in Cam's plan.

"I'm on my way home now. Do I need to wait for you? Irma promised she'd keep Beth busy until four."

Julia glanced at her watch. It was almost two o'clock. "I've got a few more errands to run but the barn isn't locked."

"One more thing." The husky timbre of Cam's voice sent shivers dancing up her arms. "What's your opinion of chocolate cake?"

"Chocolate cake is always good," Julia said cautiously.

"Good, because when I told Beth she could have some friends over to celebrate her birthday tonight, your name was the only one on the guest list."

"Really?" The word stumbled out before she could prevent it.

"Really." There was a smile in his voice. "If you don't have any plans."

None that compared to spending the evening with him and Beth.

"Should I bring something?"

"Just yourself. That's enough."

Julia hung up the phone, wishing it were true.

When had "just herself" ever been enough?

———

CAM HEARD the snap of a car door and strode out of the barn, relieved that Julia had arrived before Beth.

He could use some reinforcements. Now that the birthday gift had been delivered, he was having some doubts about the timing of his purchase. And those doubts had more to do with Julia's potential reaction to the gift than Beth's.

There was only one way to find out.

Cam stepped outside as Julia slid out of the driver's seat. Sunlight ignited threads of gold in her hair and the simple design of the dress she wore emphasized slender curves. Unaware of his presence, she tipped her face toward the sky and closed her eyes.

The carefree gesture surprised Cam. He hoped it wasn't his imagination, but her attitude seemed to be softening. And she had accepted his invitation to celebrate Beth's birthday with them. That had to mean something.

"Did you need help carrying anything in?"

Julia started at the sound of his voice but couldn't quite conceal the flash of pleasure in her eyes. Cam hoped that meant something, too. "I didn't know you were still here."

"Irma called me a few minutes ago and they're on their way back. Do you want to take a quick look before the unveiling?"

"Is Beth going to be as excited as you are?"

She was actually teasing him.

One step forward, Lord.

As they entered the barn, Julia stopped so abruptly that Cam almost bumped into her.

"That's a. . ."

"Horse." Cam strung the last word onto the sentence when her voice broke off. "Someone called the office and asked me to do an animal welfare check on some dogs at a place outside of town a few days ago. When I got there, I saw Star standing in a pen not much bigger than the kennel the owner kept his hounds in. The guy mentioned she had a one-way ticket to an auction this weekend."

Cam had been able to guess the animal's fate from there. The horse's ribs were visible beneath the filthy sorrel coat. Clumps of burrs matted its mane and tail.

A horse like Star would have been easily overlooked as a potential riding horse, but Cam had taken one look at the sweet-faced mare, up to her fetlocks in mud and waste, and dug out his checkbook.

"You bought Beth a horse."

Something in Julia's flat tone sowed more doubt. "I know Star isn't much to look at but there doesn't seem to be anything wrong with her that some TLC from a little girl won't cure. I promised Beth we'd get a horse if we found a place in the country. I didn't think it would happen this fast but she'll work out fine."

The fact that he was rambling made Cam wonder who he was trying to convince.

"What are you going to do with her?"

"Tom said there's a riding club in the area that offers lessons for beginners—"

"I mean now," Julia interrupted curtly. "Tonight."

Cam had thought that was what she meant. "I was hoping you would let us board Star here for a few days until we can put up some fencing and a shelter of our own. I'd pay you, of course—"

"You want to keep her *here?*" Julia's voice thinned and cracked on the last word.

"Just for a few days. You won't even know she's here. Beth and I will take care of everything."

"Good. Because I'm not having anything to do with it."

Cam's eyes flew to Julia's face. Her skin was bleached of color, a stark contrast to eyes as dark as uncut amethysts. She whirled around, a slight hitch in her step as she stalked toward the door.

So much for one step forward.

Cam knew he'd just taken two giant steps back.

Julia was afraid of horses.

———

"Is she really mine?"

"Hey! You're choking me." Cam gasped as Beth wrapped her arms around his neck. "And yes, she's really yours."

Beth loosened her grip. "What's her name?"

"Star." Cam's throat tightened at the look of wonder on his daughter's face. "Happy birthday, sweetheart."

"She's beautiful. Did Julia see her yet?"

That was a definite yes. "She stopped in the barn for a few seconds."

Before she'd left him standing there alone, an apology dying on his lips.

"Are we going to keep her here?"

"Not permanently." Cam quickly set Beth straight. "And it's up to you to do the work. Making sure she has fresh water. Feeding her. Grooming her."

"Work? That's going to be fun." Beth giggled when Star stretched her neck over the fence and the velvet lips nuzzled her palm. "When can I ride her?"

"Let's give her a few days to settle in to her new home first," Cam suggested. "Granna and Robert sent some gifts for you to open. Why don't we come back later to visit Star?"

"Sure." Beth gently stroked the mare's nose. "I'll get Julia."

"Ah, I don't think she's feeling very well today." Thanks to the bomb he'd dropped on her. "I'm not sure if she'll be coming over to have cake with us."

Disappointment stole the sparkle from Beth's eyes. "Maybe we could bring her a piece when we come back."

"Maybe." Cam would let Beth do the honors. He wasn't sure Julia would open the door if she saw him standing on the other side.

On the way back to the house, Cam silently berated himself for not telling Julia his plans in advance. It had seemed so logical at the time. She had a vacant barn and a fenced-in pasture. They had a horse that needed temporary lodging. A perfect match.

To make matters worse, as Beth had skipped ahead of him, Cam swore he'd heard her say, "That's two, God."

If it hadn't been for the conversation with his mother, he would have remained blissfully ignorant about what she'd meant.

And if Julia *was* part of God's plan, he'd definitely gotten in the way.

12

The warm breeze stirring the kitchen curtains promised a beautiful day.

Julia caught a glimpse of Cam and Beth as she poured a cup of coffee.

Beth was practically skipping up the driveway while her father followed at a more leisurely pace. Judging from the slouch of Cam's shoulders and his tousled hair, Julia guessed that Beth had prodded her dad out of bed earlier than he would have liked on a Saturday morning.

Near the barn, Star nibbled spears of grass while waiting for her official breakfast—a flake from one of the bales of hay stacked in a corner of the barn—to be served.

Julia was relieved that the mare seemed to have a calm, friendly disposition in spite of the way she'd been treated. Most people would have dismissed the neglected mare outright. The fact that Cam hadn't made her respect him even more.

But it still didn't mean she wanted the horse living in her barn.

Don't get involved, Julia warned herself as she stepped away from the window before they spotted her. *The only thing you agreed to provide was temporary housing.*

She knew Cam hadn't understood her reaction when she'd seen Star in the barn. Julia hadn't quite understood it herself. The only thing she did know was that her heart hadn't been prepared for the avalanche of memories that crashed over her. Or what to do with them now that she could no longer shut them out.

After Cam and Beth had gone home, she'd picked up the phone to call Cam and tell him that she couldn't come over for Beth's birthday celebration.

But when it came down to dialing the number, she couldn't do it.

Julia told herself that all she had to do was drop off the gift but Beth's shining eyes when she'd opened the door had derailed her plan.

She and Cam had maintained a polite distance throughout the evening but there'd been times she'd felt his searching gaze on her. Knowing he had an uncanny way of reading her thoughts, Julia hadn't been able to scrape up the courage to look at him.

She'd seen him raise a questioning eyebrow in her direction when Beth had opened her gift. Julia had mentioned that she worked out of her home but hadn't told Cam what she did. That was why she'd hoped Beth wouldn't notice the words *Wind River Farm Designs* embroidered on the label of her new riding jacket. But she had. And it had only added to the questions brewing in Cam's eyes.

Questions Julia wasn't ready to answer.

Fortunately, when it had come time for her to leave, Cam hadn't offered to walk her home.

Julia had been relieved. . .and disappointed.

It was those conflicting emotions that kept her inside now. Away from the man who caused them. She tackled several household projects instead. Her sink and shower were spotless. The floor mopped. She even organized her desk drawer.

Finally, Julia's curiosity got the better of her and she peeked out the window. She was surprised to see Cam and Beth standing on the opposite side of the fence from Star, watching the horse daintily finishing off her breakfast.

Something about the morose slump of Beth's shoulders set off warning bells in Julia's head. Without thinking, she pushed the door open and stepped outside to find out what was wrong.

"Good morning."

Cam turned around. In spite of the tension between them the day before, he didn't bother to hide his relief at her approach. "Good morning. Beautiful day, isn't it?" He didn't sound very convincing.

"Yes, it is." Julia's gaze moved from Cam to his daughter. "Hello, Beth. You're up bright and early this morning."

"Yeah." The girl managed a smile but Julia didn't miss the diamond-bright sheen of tears in her eyes before she looked away.

What had happened?

Julia propped her arms on the fence and did a brief but thorough assessment of the animal on the other side. Nothing appeared to be amiss.

"How is Star this morning?"

"Good." Beth's lackluster response didn't do anything to ease Julia's concern. Was it possible she wasn't happy with her new horse? In spite of the vow she'd made not to get involved, Julia had to find out why Beth seemed so dejected.

She glanced at Cam, a question in her eyes, and his helpless shrug brought her to a decision. "I came out to tell you that I put on a fresh pot of coffee and there's a pitcher of lemonade in the fridge. It's getting warm out here so I thought maybe the two of you would like something to drink."

"That would be great." Cam didn't hesitate to take Julia up on the offer. "I'll give you a hand."

"Beth? What about you?" Julia asked.

In response to her question, she received a half-hearted shrug.

Julia waited until she and Cam were out of earshot. "What's the matter?"

Cam shook his head. "I'm not sure. Beth was so excited she could hardly sleep last night. She woke me up at six-thirty raring to go, but when we got here, it was almost like she shut down or something. She talked to Star and gave her a treat but that was it. I can't even convince Beth to brush her."

Frustration leaked into Cam's voice but Julia sensed it was aimed at himself rather than his daughter.

"Is it possible that Beth is nervous?" she ventured.

"Nervous?" Cam repeated the word as if it hadn't crossed his mind. "No. She has an entire library of books about horses. How to groom them. How to take care of them. How to saddle and bridle them. Braid their manes and tails. Everything."

"But has she ever actually *done* those things?" Julia asked patiently.

Cam stepped ahead of her and held the door open. "Sure. The day camp she attended last summer offered trail rides for the girls."

Julia could guess what that experience had been like. To save time, the counselors would have had the animals all saddled and ready to go. Then the seasoned trail horses would fall in line, single file, down a path so familiar it would be like sleepwalking.

"No matter how much Beth loves horses, their size can still be intimidating to someone her age," Julia said carefully. "She doesn't know Star well enough to trust her yet. And vice versa. When it comes to horses, trust is a two-way street."

KATHRYN SPRINGER

Cam blew out a sigh. "Any suggestions?"

Julia hesitated. She had plenty of suggestions—she just wasn't sure she could share them. Not without breaking her rule.

Are you trying to tell me something, God?

She silently raised the question with an equal blend of frustration and humor. She'd opened her heart to His leading the day before and already He was taking her to places she wasn't sure she was ready to go.

"Why don't you take a glass of lemonade to Beth? I'll be out in a few minutes."

Concern, and a touch of disappointment, skimmed through Cam's eyes but he nodded.

Julia sagged against the counter as the door shut softly behind him.

"I'm not sure I can do this, Lord," she whispered.

It was the second time her thoughts had instinctively turned toward God. The moment she whispered the words, Julia felt an immediate peace as a quiet voice seemed to echo through her soul.

I'll help you.

———

"Do you want to put Star's halter on and walk her around the yard?" Cam handed Beth a glass of lemonade and propped one booted foot against the fence rail.

"I don't know." The tears welled up again.

Cam was at a loss. "It's going to be difficult for you and Star to get acquainted with a fence between you," he pointed out gently.

"I know." Beth's miserable gaze strayed to Star, who lifted inquisitive ears in their direction.

"Is Star ready for her day at the spa?" A voice sang out.

Cam turned and saw Julia. It was a good thing one of his feet was hooked over the fence rail or he might have fallen over.

The Julia striding up to them had traded in her usual wrinkle-free slacks and cashmere sweater for figure-hugging jeans and a faded cotton T-shirt. Scuffed, knee-high riding boots replaced the leather shoes she usually wore and a ball cap covered her tawny hair.

She looked. . .stunning.

Beth's eyes widened at the transformation but she recovered more quickly than Cam. "Spa treatment?"

"Sure." Julia's elusive dimple surfaced. "We'll give Star the Wind River Farm special. Bath. Shampoo. Pedicure. The whole works."

"Cool!" Beth dashed toward the barn but Cam caught up to Julia and snagged her elbow.

"You don't have to do this," he murmured. "I know that you're. . .you know."

Her expression closed. "I'm what?"

She was going to make him say it. "Afraid of horses."

"Afraid of horses."

"You looked like you were about to pass out yesterday. It may take a few days but I can make some phone calls and get someone to come out and show Beth what to do."

"I appreciate your concern, Cam, but I'll be fine."

Unconvinced, Cam searched her eyes. But instead of fear, he saw something that looked a lot like laughter.

13

"What is this called?" Julia held up a metal tool for Beth's inspection.

"A hoof pick," she responded instantly.

"Right." Julia smiled in approval. Cam had been right. Beth did know a lot about caring for horses. All she needed was the confidence to apply that knowledge.

It helped that Star patiently accepted their efforts. As Julia suspected, the mare soaked up all the attention like a tilled garden during a summer shower. The espresso-brown eyes drifted shut in a state of absolute bliss as Julia took a shedding blade and scraped away what remained of the horse's shaggy winter coat. And she stood perfectly still while they undertook the painstaking process of removing the burrs from her mane and tail.

As the morning progressed, Beth turned out to be a

willing pupil, eager to learn how to care for the horse herself.

"And what do you need to do when you're cleaning out the hooves?" Julia asked.

"Be careful not to hurt the frog."

"Star has a frog in her foot?"

Julia started at the sound of Cam's voice. Not that she'd forgotten he was there. That proved to be impossible considering he hadn't been more than two or three feet away from her for most of the morning. Not surprisingly, he was as gentle and patient with the mare as he was with his daughter.

Several times, Julia had felt his gaze settle on her but she'd been careful not to make eye contact. Too dangerous. She'd seen the questions in his eyes when she'd retrieved her old grooming bucket from the tack room, but fortunately they'd been so busy that he hadn't had the chance to voice any of them.

She still couldn't believe he'd thought she was afraid of horses.

Tell him.

Julia shook the thought away. She couldn't. Not yet. Maybe not ever.

Beth giggled. "The frog is part of the hoof, Dad."

"I think you'll have to lend me some of those books Granna gave you." Their eyes met over Beth's head and Cam winked at her. Julia felt the impact clear down to her toes.

Flustered, she knelt down, talking to Star in a reassuring voice as she ran her hand down one fetlock. The horse obediently picked up her foot.

"Good girl."

In response to Julia's praise, Star swung her head around and gently lipped Julia's hair.

"Hey, none of that now," she admonished.

Cam chuckled. "She must like the smell of jasmine."

He recognized the scent she wore? Julia's heart skipped a few beats. She flinched and Star's ears flattened at the sudden movement. Giving the horse's flank a quick, reassuring pat, she rose to her feet, praying that the muscles in her leg would cooperate. She didn't want to end up falling into Cam's arms.

Or did she?

"Beth—" Julia pushed the word out. "I've got some clean rags in the tack room. Could you get them? I think we're almost finished here."

At least *she* was.

"Sure." Beth obeyed in a flash.

Julia immediately realized her mistake. Now she was alone with Cam.

"Julia." The husky scrape of his voice sent a shiver up her arms. "Thank you. I seem to be saying that a lot lately, don't I? But—"

Julia didn't wait for him to finish the sentence. "Beth must be having trouble finding the rags. I better help her."

There was no sign of the girl in the tack room but a

knot formed in Julia's stomach when she saw another door standing wide open.

"I'm in here!"

There was no mistaking the excitement in Beth's voice. Which caused a second knot to form in Julia's stomach. She swallowed hard and entered the room, knowing exactly what she'd see inside.

Cam, who'd followed her—again—stopped short in the doorway.

"Who won all these trophies?" Beth pointed to the glass cases lining the walls.

Out of the corner of her eye, Julia saw the expression of disbelief on Cam's face. Somehow, that made it even more difficult to tell the truth. Not that she had a choice now.

"I did."

———

I DID.

The words barely registered over the rushing sound in Cam's head. His emotions shifting to autopilot, he walked into the spacious room. With its leather furniture and paneled walls, it looked more like the kind of comfortable, well-appointed office a person would find in a home rather than a barn.

Beth pointed to a framed photograph above the sofa. "Is this your horse, Julia?"

Instead of denying it, as Cam expected her to, Julia gave a curt nod.

"What's her name?"

For a moment, Cam didn't think she would answer. And then, "Her registered name was A Midsummer Night's Dream but her barn name was Summer."

"Where is she now?"

"Beth?" Cam jumped into the conversation when he saw Julia pale. "It's time to clean up, remember?"

Beth took one look at Julia's stricken expression and bobbed her head in agreement. "Okay."

"How about giving Star a treat for being so patient during her bath?" Cam fished a carrot stick out of his pocket. "We'll be right there."

Beth slanted a worried look at Julia before she picked up the grain bucket and headed for the door.

Cam knew he should follow Beth and let Julia shut the door on her past, but he stepped closer to get a better view of the photograph instead.

Wearing a stylish tuxedo jacket, tan riding breeches and knee-high boots, Julia looked perfectly at ease astride an ebony horse. Her honey-blond hair framed features that were slightly younger. Softer. But it was the expression on Julia's face that Cam couldn't tear his gaze away from.

She looked happy. As if there wasn't anywhere else in the world that she would rather be.

All morning Cam had been quietly amazed at the ease with which Julia handled both Star and his daughter. She'd known exactly what to do, as if she'd done it a thousand times. Now he knew why.

He shook his head. "No wonder you laughed at me for thinking you were afraid of horses."

"I didn't laugh."

Cam gave her a skeptical glance. "Maybe not on the outside."

A ghost of a smile touched her lips. "Like I told Beth—it was a long time ago." She shrugged. "A lifetime ago."

"But—"

"I used to ride. I don't anymore. End of story." Without a backward glance—at him or the reminders of her past—Julia slipped from the room.

Cam knew it wasn't the end of the story. But would she ever trust him enough to tell it?

14

"**J**ulia! We're here!"

A familiar woof accompanied Beth's cheerful greeting.

Julia couldn't prevent a smile. Right on time.

Ever since the day she'd supervised Star's makeover, Julia now found herself part of the Delaneys' daily routine. After school, Beth would stop in to say hello before going to the barn to feed Star, deliver fresh water, and muck out the stall.

The first time she'd shown up, Julia had been a little taken aback by the unannounced visit. Especially when Belle had scooted in and made herself at home on the rug in front of the sink while Beth entertained Julia with stories from her school day. By the third visit, Beth was comfortable enough to sneak a peek in the cookie jar on the counter.

Julia made sure she kept it filled.

She'd started to look forward to Beth's arrival. It was Cam's daily visit she tried to avoid. After supper, he would supervise Beth while she and Star took a sedate walk around the pasture. His laughter inevitably drew Julia to the window, where she would linger a moment to watch Beth, silently correcting her posture.

Back straight. Heels down. Hands low. Eyes forward.

Every time she was tempted to go outside and help Beth with her equitation, the man leaning against the fence stopped her.

Julia hadn't known she was such a coward.

Only this time she wasn't avoiding Cam because she was haunted by the past. No. This time she was afraid of the future.

"Look what I got at school today." Beth kicked off her boots on the rug inside the door and skidded into the kitchen, waving a bright green piece of paper.

Julia pointed to the cookie jar as she took the flyer. It was an advertisement for the Blue Ribbon Rendezvous, an annual horse show sponsored by a local riding club. She didn't need to read the rest to know what it would say.

Wind River Farm had once hosted the event.

"This is in two weeks."

"That's a lot of time, right?" Beth broke off a piece of cookie and fed it to Belle.

Julia looked over the list of events again. Some of

them were geared for beginning riders but she couldn't help but compare Star to the horses Beth would be competing against.

"Are you sure you don't want to wait another month? There will be other shows this summer."

"Don't you think we're ready?" The silent appeal in Beth's eyes arrowed straight to Julia's heart. "Dad said that I should try because the show is just for fun."

Just for fun. Julia wished she had heard those words at Beth's age. She eased her grip on the past. Tried to remember what was important.

"He's right. You and Star will do fine." Julia handed her back the flyer and was gifted with a bright smile. "What events do you want to enter?"

"All of them."

"I knew you were going to say that." Julia laughed and gave Beth an impulsive hug.

To her amazement, Beth clung to her. "Come on. Let's go."

"Go where?"

Beth snitched another cookie. "To the barn. We've got a lot of work to do before the show. I have no idea what I'm doing."

That, Julia thought, made two of them.

But she grabbed her boots, just the same.

Everything went well until Star balked at the first jump.

Julia hurried forward, bracing herself for the

inevitable as Beth's feet came out of the irons and she pitched forward.

By the time she reached them, Beth had caught herself from catapulting over Star's head. The horse, however, was still dancing in place, eyes rolling suspiciously at the unfamiliar object in her path.

"She's afraid of it," Beth said, shaken by the close call.

Julia put a soothing hand on Star's neck and the other on Beth's knee. "That's because you told her to be."

"Me?" The word came out in a squeak.

Julia smiled. "It's easy to think the horses are the ones that are brave and in charge because they're so big. But even though you're a team, Star has to trust that *you* are the one in charge. As you got closer to the jump, your posture changed. You tensed up and pulled back on the reins. Those were signals to Star that she should be afraid, too."

"I am kind of afraid of falling," Beth admitted in a small voice.

"You are going to fall."

Beth's eyes widened and Julia laughed. "It's inevitable, sweetheart. Everyone falls off at some point. The important thing is to get back on again."

Not that she'd taken her own advice.

"Okay." Beth eyed the jump apprehensively, not as inspired by the pep talk as Julia hoped she'd be.

"Go ahead and show Star there's nothing to be afraid of."

"Julia?"

"Yes?"

"Will you show her first?"

———

CAM WALKED over the rise just in time to see Julia and Star sail over a low jump set up in the pasture. The muscles under Star's glossy coat rippled as if an invisible current flowed beneath them.

Julia's delighted laugh danced in the background of Beth's exuberant applause.

His heart locked up at the sound and he raised his hand to wave as the horse swung around. But instead of returning to the gate, Julia turned Star toward the woods on the other side of the field and they cantered away.

Beth raced up to him. "Isn't she amazing, Dad?"

Amazing. Unpredictable. Irresistible. Beautiful.

Cam couldn't decide which description fit the best.

"I guess that's the reason she won all those trophies." He pulled Beth against him and gave her a fierce hug.

Beth giggled. "I was talking about Star, Dad, not Julia."

Oops. Busted. Cam felt his face grow warm. "She's amazing, too. Why did Julia come out to help you?"

"Because I asked her," Beth said simply.

Mmm. Maybe he should have tried that. Every evening when he walked over to Wind River Farm to watch Beth ride, Julia stayed in the house, holed up like a groundhog in February. He'd been wondering how to coax her out of hiding.

"I told Julia about the show. It's in two weeks but she thinks we'll be ready by then. But I couldn't get Star to go over the jump and Julia said it was because she knew I was afraid."

Which was why Julia had taken Star over the jump first.

I used to ride. I don't anymore. End of story.

Cam's throat tightened. He'd already come to the conclusion that he and Julia needed to talk. If he could ever get her alone.

While they waited for Julia to return, Beth shared more details about the show. It was Mother's Day weekend. Some of the girls from school were entering, too. She needed riding clothes. They would have to rent a trailer.

Cam's head was beginning to swim when Beth broke off mid-sentence, a frown settling between her brows. "Do you think they're okay? Where did they go?"

Cam's gaze drifted to the opening in the trees where Julia and Star had disappeared. More than twenty minutes had already gone by. "I'm sure they're fine. Why don't you go up to the house and finish your homework? I'll take care of Star when they get back."

"Okay." Fortunately, Beth was too exhausted to argue. "Tell Julia I'll see her tomorrow."

Another half hour went by and the sun had slipped behind the trees when Cam heard the soft, rhythmic thud of hoofbeats in the pasture. Relief poured through him. He'd been close to sending out a search party.

Cam took one look at Julia as she led Star into the barn and knew they hadn't taken a leisurely trail ride. Julia's hair was tousled and damp; her porcelain skin glowed with perspiration. She looked as if she'd been strapped to the back of a missile.

And loved every minute of it.

Neither of them said a word while Cam unfastened Star's bridle and Julia removed the saddle.

"Beth?" she finally asked.

"I sent her home to shower and finish her homework."

A flash of guilt crossed Julia's face. "I guess I lost track of the time."

"I didn't think time existed when a person traveled at the speed of light," Cam said mildly.

Julia caught her lower lip between her teeth, unable to deny it. "I wouldn't push Star too hard."

"I know that. I was teasing you."

A smile tipped Julia's lips and she gave Star's neck an affectionate pat before turning her out. Cam rolled his eyes. He was jealous of a horse. Pathetic.

Julia watched the horse trot into the pasture, one hand idly massaging her hip. "She's a good horse, Cam.

Smart. Eager to please. She and Beth will make a good team."

"Beth told me about the show. It was nice of you to help her, even though, knowing my daughter, she probably didn't give you much of a choice."

"They'll do fine." Julia took a step toward the door. And then another.

It occurred to Cam that he'd gotten the very thing he'd been hoping for. A chance to talk with Julia alone.

"Good night." A third step.

One more and she'd be beyond his reach. Again. Cam decided to take a risk.

"Why did you give up something you love?"

15

J ulia found herself wishing Cam hadn't waited for her to return to the barn after her impulsive ride.

"I don't love it anymore."

"I don't believe you."

As if he didn't trust her not to make a break for it, Cam crossed the distance between them. Strong hands closed around her arms, but instead of making her feel trapped, his grip was warm. Comforting.

The gentle touch made her want to lean against his chest and draw from his strength. Even knowing that she didn't deserve it.

"Why did you give up riding? Did it have something to do with the accident?"

"You know about that?" Julia didn't know why it surprised her. Lucy or Irma Robertson had probably filled him in on all the grim details the minute he'd bought the house next door.

"I know you got hurt and I'm guessing it had something to do with horses. Did the doctors advise you not to ride? Is that it?"

"No, that isn't it." Julia twisted away from him. "I can ride. I just don't *want* to. Sometimes horses are a phase. Something a person outgrows."

"That may be true, but not for you. I saw the look on your face when you took Star over that jump tonight. You looked like a woman who was exactly where she wanted to be."

She refused to cry. Not in front of Cam. She'd managed to contain her tears for four years; she could hold them back a little longer.

"It's in the past."

"I don't think it is. I think whatever happened is something you carry every day." Cam reached up and brushed back the damp strands of hair from her cheek. "Tell me, Julia. *Trust* me."

Julia stared up at him.

Trust. It sounded so simple. Did Cam know he was asking the impossible?

"Whatever this is about, you don't have to go through it alone."

Julia wished that were true. But once Cam knew what she'd done—what she was capable of—she could stop dreaming about a future that included him and Beth.

Maybe that was reason enough to tell him.

She nodded, acutely aware of Cam's arm around her as he led her to the sofa in the trophy room.

A fitting place, Julia thought bitterly. Her emotions shut down when she looked at the photo of her and Summer on the wall. That girl was a stranger to her now. Acknowledging that made it easier to face the past. Made it seem as if she were a spectator rather than a participant.

"Summer and I were signed up for a riding competition in Kentucky one weekend but a storm came through and the course turned to mud." Without closing her eyes, Julia could feel the pelting rain. Hear the low keen of the wind. "Some of the riders withdrew but people from the Olympic equestrian team were there and Mom had heard a rumor my name was being tossed around.

"Laine, one of the other competitors, tried to convince the judges to cancel the event. I knew my mother wanted me to compete so I told them that completing the course depended on the skill of the rider more than the terrain." The arrogance of the assertion still seared Julia's conscience. "Laine and I got to the second fence at the same time but her horse, Diamond, slipped and collided with Summer. That's all I remember.

"I woke up in the ICU two days later. Then came three months of rehab, a broken engagement, and the end of my riding career." Julia paused. "I knew everyone blamed me. Wind River Farm was one of the major sponsors so people assumed that's why the judges listened to me and not Laine. If I'd backed her up. . ."

Julia's voice trailed off and when Cam reached for her hand again, she pulled away.

———

THE SELF-RECRIMINATION in Julia's tone, the empty look in her eyes, told Cam the rest of the story.

Why hadn't he put the clues together until now? The vacant stalls. Julia's reaction to Star. The walls she'd built around her heart. They all added up to one thing.

Guilt.

Cam recognized the symptoms. He'd dealt with those feelings after Laurel died.

Julia blamed herself for what had happened that day. She hadn't forgiven herself for what had happened that day.

"Laine?" He had to ask. Had to know if that was part of it.

"She didn't get hurt. But Diamond. . .the vet had to put him down. Laine loved that horse. . . like I loved Summer." Julia stared, unseeing, at the trophies on the wall. "I wanted to prove myself. Wanted to win. But instead, I lost. Everything."

From her tone, it was clear Julia believed that she'd deserved it.

"What happened when you got home?" Cam

remembered Lucy saying something about Tara Windham not coming home much after the accident.

"Mom took a job teaching riding lessons at a private school out of state. She'd sold Summer while I was in rehab."

Another wound. And one, Cam guessed, that still hadn't healed.

Help me find the right words, Lord.

"You have to forgive yourself. It's the only way you can put the past to rest and move forward." He paused, knowing that in this situation, he could speak from experience. "I blamed myself when my wife died. Laurel had asked me to give her a ride to the restaurant and I told her I didn't have time. If I would have gone five minutes out of my way, she might still be alive."

"That wasn't your fault. You didn't know what would happen."

"Neither did you." Cam saw the impact the words had on Julia. "Maybe that's the reason your mom left. She might still be battling guilt because she pushed you to enter the competition that day."

Julia immediately began to shake her head. Short, jerky little shakes that looked as if someone was asking questions she didn't want to answer. "No. Mom couldn't settle for anything less than the best. When I couldn't win anymore, she wanted to find someone who could."

"Or she couldn't stay on the farm and be reminded every day of what you'd lost," Cam said softly. "I know that guilt ate me up inside until I turned everything over to God. The whole angry, grieving mess inside of me. It made all the difference. He's the only one who can bring something good out of our messes. And Julia, that's what He wants to do for you. Trust Him."

Trust in the Lord.

The verse from Beth's devotional book.

Why wasn't she surprised? Lately, no matter what she was doing, it shimmered below the surface of her thoughts like background music.

Julia wanted to trust. Was trying to trust. But the changes God was making in her heart wouldn't change the consequences of the mistake she'd made that day.

"Julia, I care about you. Beth cares about you." Cam's voice roughened with the intensity of his feelings. "I didn't think I'd ever feel this way again, but—"

"Wait." Julia stopped Cam before he went any further. "I told you that after the accident, my fiancé broke up with me."

"If the guy dumped you because you got hurt then you were better off without him."

Julia rose to her feet and wrapped her arms around her middle. She had to tell him everything, even knowing it would form a barrier between them. One that would prevent his feelings from becoming deeper.

Unfortunately, it was too late for her.

"He left when he found out that my injuries were so significant that the doctor believed it would be difficult —if not impossible—for me to get pregnant."

Julia saw Cam's eyes darken with denial as her words sank in.

She waited. One heartbeat of silence stretched into two.

It was the reaction she'd expected but she hadn't known how much it would hurt.

"It doesn't matter, Julia."

"It does to me." And it would to him. Maybe not right away. But when it happened, Julia knew her heart wouldn't hold up under the weight of Cam's regret. Or pity.

He was an amazing father. If he fell in love again. . . married again. . .he would want more children. And Beth would be a wonderful big sister.

Julia wouldn't take that away from them.

Cam stared out the window, hoping to catch a glimpse of Julia as she supervised Beth's evening riding lesson.

A glimpse had to be enough. For now.

He'd asked Julia for the truth and yet hadn't been prepared for its impact. In the split second of silence that followed her stunning disclosure, a chasm had opened up between them.

Julia had been honest with him but Cam hadn't been honest with himself or the depth of his feelings. Somewhere along the way, he had fallen in love with her. The realization had broadsided his heart. By the time he regained consciousness, Julia had misinterpreted his silence for doubt.

He'd spent several sleepless nights since then asking God what to do.

Cam was well acquainted with loss. He knew that

Julia had to choose to turn her pain over to the only One who could set her free her from the burden she'd been carrying.

The front door slammed and Cam frowned as he stepped into the hall to see what the commotion was about.

"Daddy!" Beth skidded toward him.

Cam caught her in his arms, quickly checking knees and elbows for scrapes. Other than the tears streaming down his daughter's face, there didn't seem to be any visible signs of injury.

"What happened, Tig?"

"Is Julia mad at me? Did I do something wrong?"

Dread pooled in Cam's stomach. Although he and Julia hadn't spoken since the night in the barn, he couldn't believe Julia would say or do anything to intentionally hurt Beth.

"I'm sure you didn't do anything wrong."

"But Julia said. . ." Beth gasped out the words. "She isn't coming to the show with us this weekend. She has other p-plans." She burrowed her face against his chest.

Cam gathered her closer and closed his eyes. He should have seen this coming. Julia had never said she would attend the show. Guilt had forced her into a self-imposed exile after the accident. It was one thing to help Beth prepare for the horse show behind the scenes, safe within the shelter of her own property. Another to expose herself to the stares and speculation of the same people who had once cheered for her from the stands.

"It's all right, Beth. I'll be there to help you."

"You don't understand," Beth wailed. "It's Mother's Day and all the riders are supposed to give a rose to their moms. If Julia isn't there, how am I supposed to give her one?"

Mother's Day roses.

He drew Beth to the couch in the living room and she melted against him.

"Julia isn't your mom, sweetheart."

Beth sniffled. "She would be if you got married."

The bones in Cam's body liquefied, making him glad he was sitting down. "It's not always that easy."

"But she likes you and you like her. I can tell." Fresh tears leaked out the corners of Beth's eyes. "But maybe she doesn't like me anymore."

"Julia likes you very much."

"Then why won't she come with us?"

Cam sent up a silent SOS. He didn't want to break a confidence, but Beth needed to know there was a reason for Julia's decision. "Do you remember how sad we were after Mom died?"

Beth nodded. "My heart hurt all the time."

Cam's throat tightened. "So did mine."

"Did Julia's mom die?"

"No," Cam said swiftly. "But losing someone isn't the only thing that can make a person sad. Julia was hurt in a riding accident a few years ago and she had to give up a lot of the things she wanted to do."

"She doesn't look hurt."

"Not on the outside, but I think her heart still hurts, just like ours did. We have to give Julia time. Not push her to do things she isn't ready for yet, like the horse show."

Or risking her heart again.

"You and I both know that God is the only One who can heal people on the inside." Cam took a deep breath but it didn't ease the weight pressing against his heart. "He helped us and we have to believe He'll help Julia, too."

———

"You're going to let me use that one?"

Julia smiled at the awestruck look on Beth's face.

Her mother had sold most of the tack before she'd moved away, but for some reason had left the show saddle Julia had saved an entire year to buy when she was about Beth's age.

"If you'd like. It needs a good cleaning, though." Julia set the saddle down on the blanket spread out in the grass.

"Are you kidding?" Beth's fingers traced the satin-smooth leather. "I love it."

"There's a matching bridle, too."

"Was it Summer's?"

"Yes."

Julia wasn't surprised by the question. Summer had become a favorite topic when she and Beth got together in the evenings to prepare for the upcoming show. What had come as a surprise was that Julia no longer minded talking about the horse that had been her best friend and confidante. Another one of the amazing changes that had bloomed out of the conversations she'd been having with God recently.

Julia had always shied away from remembering the past, but in shutting out the painful memories, she'd closed out the good ones, as well.

Beth picked up a soft cloth and followed Julia's lead, rubbing oil into the leather. "Summer liked to jump, didn't she? I can tell because she looks happy in the pictures."

Julia wondered how many people would think it strange to hear a horse described as happy. She, on the other hand, understood perfectly. "It was her favorite."

"Star likes it, too. Dad said he's going to take a lot of pictures of us on Saturday."

Julia tensed.

As the day of the show drew closer, she'd wondered if Beth would try to convince her to change her mind about accompanying them.

"Dad and I are going out for ice cream tonight. Do you want to come?"

Julia blinked at the sudden change in topic even as the thought of spending time with Cam caused her pulse to skip a beat. Ever since she'd told him about the accident, he had watched Beth's riding lessons from the fence that bordered the two properties.

Julia told herself—repeatedly—that she didn't mind. Cam had encouraged her to forgive herself for the mistakes she'd made, but it wouldn't change the high price she'd paid for them. A price she couldn't ask Cam to pay, too.

"I can't." Julia refused to let her gaze drift to the house across the pasture. "I have a lot of work to finish by Friday."

As the temperature began to climb and the number of equine events increased, it was always a challenge to keep up with the orders for show clothes that came in.

"Okay."

Okay? Julia felt a pinch of disappointment that Beth didn't seem, well, more disappointed.

A bell clanged and Belle's ears lifted at the sound. Apparently, Cam had discovered that his daughter's ingenious device for calling the dog home worked well for eleven-year-old girls, too.

"I think Dad is ready to go." Beth bit her lip, obviously torn between going out for ice cream or staying to clean tack.

Julia hid a smile. Only a girl who loved horses would look so conflicted. "Go ahead. I'll finish up here."

"You're going to put everything back in the barn, right?"

Julia found the question a bit odd. "Right."

"Okay." Beth bent down and gave her a quick hug. "See you tomorrow."

Julia focused on the task, pretending not to notice when Cam's car cruised past. Half an hour later, she anchored the saddle against one hip and carried it back to the barn. It was strange, but she'd noticed that the more she worked with Star, the better her leg felt.

The mare rattled the stall door when Julia entered the building.

"As if you don't get enough attention." Julia's laughter faded when she saw an enormous blue ribbon fashioned out of cardboard and bright blue tissue paper. But it was the words carefully printed at the top of the ribbon, spelled out in silver glitter, that stole her breath.

Best Neighbor.

The gesture was unexpected. Sweet. And so. . .Beth.

Julia knew it should have made her smile, but instead her vision blurred as she faced the truth.

She wanted to be more than a neighbor.

"What's the grin for?" Cam sat down on the swing next to Beth. "Did you get extra chocolate chips in your chocolate-chip ice cream?"

"Nope." She rolled her tongue around the base of the cone to catch a drip. "Just because."

Just because.

Cam's eyes narrowed.

Why didn't he believe her?

When Beth came home after her riding lesson, she'd told him that Julia had turned down her invitation to go out for ice cream. It was the cheerful tone in which she'd said it that struck Cam as odd. For someone who loved to spend time with Julia, he would have expected Beth's mood to reflect her disappointment.

He'd been more than a little disappointed himself.

"Because—" he prompted.

Beth's freckles began to glow.

"Okay." Cam crossed his arms. "What did you do?"

"Do?"

"Yes, do. The freckles don't lie. You've been up to something."

Beth became fascinated by the clouds that drifted over the park.

"Now your ears are pink." Cam braced himself. "Spill it."

"I made Julia a blue ribbon that said *Best Neighbor* and I hung it in the barn where she would find it," Beth admitted in a rush.

"You do remember what I said—" Cam resisted the urge to add the words *two days ago* "—that we have to pray for Julia."

"I did pray."

"And let *God* work in her heart." He didn't resist the urge to emphasize the word *God*. "Remember?"

"I remember." Beth's forehead puckered. Cam sensed a "but" coming. "But—" He hid a smile. "Granna says that sometimes God wants us to be His hands on earth."

His mother did say that. Frequently. In fact, one of Claire Delaney Owens's favorite sayings was, "God likes to use our arms to hug people."

"She's right." Cam couldn't deny it.

"That's what I remembered when I prayed about Julia." Beth peeked up at him through a fringe of silky copper bangs. "I know that God is working on Julia's inside, but it doesn't mean we can't do something on her outside, does it?"

The question punched the air out of Cam's lungs.

Out of the mouths of babes. Or in this case, precocious eleven-year-old girls!

He'd decided that giving Julia time to work through the past was the best decision. Knew that grief and guilt could paralyze a person's faith. But now, looking back, Cam realized it had been his mother's patience, coupled with the simple, loving acts of kindness from fellow believers, that had helped him find his way out of the darkness after Laurel died.

Cam hadn't wanted to get in God's way, but what if Beth was right? Julia had been alone for a long time. Maybe instead of space, she needed someone to care enough to trespass over her boundaries.

"So the blue ribbon you made was for Julia's. . .outside?" Cam guessed.

"She hasn't gotten one for a while. I thought she'd like it."

The sparkle in her eyes warned Cam she had something else up her little pink sleeve. "Let me guess. You have another idea."

Beth reached into her backpack and presented him with a bright pink notebook and a glitter-filled pen. "It's all in here."

Cam wasn't sure whether to feel proud or terrified by the fact that she had a written plan.

He thumbed open the cover and sucked in an

astonished breath when he saw the next idea on her list. "Beth, I don't think this one is possible."

"But that's the best one," Beth said serenely. "And I'm already working on it." She tapped the tip of the pen against number three to refocus his attention. "You can be in charge of this one."

Cam didn't feel as if he were in charge at all.

But on second thought, maybe that was a good thing.

———

"JULIA?"

Julia heard the kitchen door rattle and glanced at her watch.

Four o'clock.

Where had the day gone?

She'd sat down at the sewing machine right after breakfast and worked straight through lunch. When Julia had agreed to fill the order, she hadn't anticipated her evenings being taken up with riding lessons and all the last-minute details that needed attention before a show.

"I'll be down in a few minutes."

"Okay." Beth sang out the word and Julia's spirits lifted.

Order or not, she didn't mind giving up an evening for Beth.

Julia flipped off the light on the sewing machine and straightened up her work space.

A loud thump rattled the walls.

"What's going on down there?" she called. "Is Belle rearranging the living-room furniture again?"

"No." A giggle followed. "Can I turn the radio on, Julia?"

"I suppose so."

Seconds later, a familiar country tune spilled out of the speakers, filling every nook and cranny in the house.

More thumps. Maybe Belle and Beth were practicing line dancing while they waited for her.

Hopefully they wouldn't expect her to join in, Julia thought as she pushed her tired limbs down the stairs and rounded the corner into the kitchen.

The transformed kitchen.

"Surprise!" Beth grinned as Julia struggled to take in the change in her surroundings.

A red and white checkered cloth had replaced the square of beige linen that normally covered the table. Colorful, mismatched ceramic bowls surrounded a trio of chunky candles.

"What is all this?"

Beth grinned. "Supper!"

"We thought you might need a break from cooking."

Julia's breath stalled as Cam appeared in her line of vision. The fact they hadn't spoken for several days didn't lessen the impact of seeing him face-to-face.

"Are you surprised?" Beth tugged her toward the table.

"Yes." Surprised. Speechless. Shaken. Julia wasn't sure which one to choose.

"I'll sit here." Beth claimed one of the chairs and pointed to the opposite side of the table. "You can have that one."

Which put her right next to Cam. Close enough that if she moved a fraction of an inch, their shoulders would be touching. As it was, she could smell the tangy scent of his cologne.

"Do you mind if I say grace?" Cam looked at her and Julia's heart lifted at the word.

Yes. Grace.

"We hold hands when we pray." Beth reached across the table.

Julia could only nod mutely as Cam's fingers wove through hers. She felt the warmth and strength of his hand. And didn't want to let go.

"Lord, we thank You for your many blessings. For this food. For friends and family. But most of all, for Your love for us."

"And that You answer our prayers," Beth added in a whisper.

Cam cleared his throat. "And that You answer our prayers."

"So." Julia fumbled with the fork next to her plate. "What's the special occasion? The horse show tomorrow?"

"No." Beth's pigtails swung in time with the decisive shake of her head. "This."

Julia frowned. "This?"

"Uh-huh." Beth looked at her father. "Right, Dad?"

"Right."

Cam smiled as if no further explanation was necessary.

And maybe it wasn't.

———

Cam took the dishes over to the sink and rinsed them off. From his vantage point at the window, he could see Beth towing Julia toward the barn, chattering all the way.

All afternoon, when he should have been considering what to do about the rubber ball that Sean O'Grady's chocolate Lab had swallowed, Cam was wondering if their plan would backfire.

Beth had mentioned that Julia was trying to finish a special order for a customer. Her idea—number three on the list—had been to take Julia out for pizza. Cam figured she would come up with a reason to decline the invitation. That left one option. If Julia wouldn't go to a restaurant, the restaurant would have to come to Julia.

Right up until the moment he'd lit the candles, Cam resisted the urge to make a quick getaway. But all his fears had been put to rest when Julia saw the table set for three.

Dinner seemed like such a simple thing. But when was the last time someone had gone out of their way to make Julia feel special? Loved?

Thank You, Lord, that Beth saw what I didn't.

No wonder Jesus had encouraged His disciples to have the faith of a child.

He dried his hands off on the towel and stepped outside.

The trailer he'd rented to take Star to the show in the morning was parked next to the barn. Washed, waxed and ready to go the next morning.

Every night, Beth had prayed that Julia would come to the show, but so far Cam had seen no evidence that she was going to change her mind. It was a struggle. He knew he should prepare his daughter for the possibility that Julia wouldn't show up, but he didn't want to crush her simple but steadfast faith, either.

You're in control, Lord. Beth and I are doing what we can on the outside and we'll trust that You're working in Julia's heart.

"Don't look at me like that. I came here to think. There's nothing unusual about that."

But maybe, Julia thought when Belle barked at her—for the third time in less than a minute—there *was* something unusual about talking to a dog. While perched on the branch of a tree. At seven o'clock in the morning.

What was wrong with this picture?

Julia glanced at her watch. Again. The first event would be starting in a little over an hour.

Belle barked again.

"Fine. You win." Julia began to climb down, remembering the day that Cam had discovered her in the tree.

The day he'd almost kissed her.

Julia groaned.

What was the point in running away if your troubled thoughts came along for the ride?

She'd gone for a walk along the river, hoping the peaceful surroundings would make her feel, well, peaceful. Instead, as the minutes ticked by, Julia's restlessness only increased.

"I'm nervous, Julia," Beth had confided while they finished packing the last of the equipment the night before. "Will you pray for me?"

The question had scooped out a chunk of Julia's heart. "Of course, I will. You and Star will do great. All you have to remember is to have fun."

Now Julia imagined the announcer taking his place in the booth. The nervous energy of the horses shifting in the stalls. The organized chaos of the riders as they prepared for the first event.

Beth was probably terrified.

Julia closed her eyes.

I know You're with Beth, Lord. Remind her of that. Help her not to be afraid....

I'm with you, too.

The thought cut a shimmering path through the center of Julia's prayer. Exposing her own doubts and fears. Revealing the truth. She wasn't afraid of the stares or the whispers behind her back. She was afraid to trust her feelings for Cam. Afraid to risk her heart again.

She hadn't believed him when he'd told her the past didn't matter. Hadn't believed that someone could care about her. . .

But if she could trust God to heal the past, couldn't she trust Him with her future, too?

I don't deserve it, Lord. Cam said You make beautiful things out of the messes we make. I want to believe that You've been looking out for me. Loving me.

The words tumbled through Julia's mind as she took a shortcut through the woods that came out near the mailboxes.

What greeted her was a large, hand-painted sign fastened to a tree at the end of Cam's driveway.

Second Chance Farm.

The crooked letters were rose-petal pink.

Julia laughed out loud. Lifted her face to the sky.

"I believe you," she said.

Now she had to tell Cam the same thing.

———

The rose ceremony.

Julia's feet turned to lead.

How could she have forgotten the Blue Ribbon Rendezvous tradition? During the lunch break, the riders would stop in front of the outdoor bleachers, dismount and present their mothers with a long-stemmed rose. The women would then take their place on the horses while their daughters or sons led them around the ring.

You can do this, she told herself. For Beth and Cam.

"Bethany Delaney from Second Chance Farm."

Julia heard the announcement and paused, wondering if Cam would be the one accepting the flower.

Someone suddenly grabbed her hand and began to pull her through the crowd.

"Cam!" Julia tried to dig in her heels. "What are you doing?"

"Hurry up. Beth is waiting for you."

"Waiting for me? How did you know I'd be here?"

"Where else would you be?" Cam grinned. "Beth has been praying. And so have I."

Before Julia could react to that startling bit of news, Cam's hands framed her face and he kissed her.

The scattered applause brought her back to reality and they broke apart. Cam didn't look the least bit repentant.

"Go on." He nudged her forward. "It's your turn."

Her turn.

For the first time in a long time, Julia let herself believe it.

She slipped through the fence and several of the mothers moved aside to make room for her.

Julia's heart almost burst when she saw Beth and Star crossing the ring toward her.

Only it wasn't Star she was leading.

Julia's fingers covered her mouth as the coal-black mare lifted her ears and nickered softly.

. . .

Summer.

But how. . .

Tears leaked from the corners of Julia's eyes as Beth stopped in front of her and presented her with a long-stemmed rose.

In a daze, Julia put her foot in the saddle and swung her leg over Summer's back. By the time they exited the ring a few minutes later, she couldn't see a thing.

"Hey." Cam was there, reaching for her. "I hope these are happy tears."

"How?" Julia stumbled over the word.

"It was all Beth's idea but we had some help from an inside source."

Through her tears, Julia saw a blurred shape step closer.

She blinked them away and recognized a familiar face. *"Mom?"*

Tara Windham nodded a little uncertainly but smiled when her gaze slid to Beth. "I got a call from a junior detective last week, asking if I knew how to find Summer. And then Cam came on the line and explained that you'd tried to find her a long time ago." Her mother looked away. "After the accident, when you were in the hospital, you said you didn't want any reminders of what had happened. I thought Summer would be one of them. I wasn't trying to hurt you, Julia. I thought I was helping. I thought Summer would be a constant reminder that you'd lost your dreams. Your passion."

Not lost, Julia thought. Buried beneath a layer of guilt. And it had taken Beth and Cam to help her find it again.

"I didn't think I deserved to own a horse," Julia whispered, laying her head against Summer's neck.

"What you didn't deserve was what happened that day."

Julia was stunned to see her mother's eyes fill with tears. Was it possible Cam had been right when he'd suggested that her mother had been wrestling with guilt, too?

"Your mother contacted some people and traced Summer to a stable in lower Michigan," Cam explained. "The owner agreed to sell her after I explained the situation, but we had no idea how to get Summer here in time for the show."

"*You* brought her here?" Julia looked at her mother in amazement.

"I was told that, and I quote, 'time is of the essence.'" Tara winked at Beth, who grinned.

"Are you surprised?" Beth hopped back and forth from one foot to the other, unable to contain her excitement. "I wanted to tell you last night but Dad said it would be better if we surprised you today when I gave you the rose."

"But how did you know I'd be here?"

"I prayed that you would talk to God about it," Beth said simply.

Cam reached for her hand, as if he knew that she needed something to hold on to.

She'd listened to her heart. Listened to God. And He'd brought her here.

"I'm. . ." Julia choked on a laugh as Summer nudged her arm, as if seeking some attention of her own. "I still can't believe you found her. *Why* did you find her?"

Beth rolled her eyes, as if she couldn't believe Julia had to ask.

"Because we love you, silly."

Julia glanced at Cam, almost afraid to witness his response to Beth's announcement.

"She's right. As always." Cam pulled Julia into his arms. Whispered in her ear. "We love you, silly."

EPILOGUE

"I can't see a thing!" Julia laughed, putting her fingers to the bandana that Beth had placed over her eyes.

"That's the point." Beth giggled.

"No peeking, either, or you'll ruin the surprise." Cam's hand rested on the small of Julia's back as he guided her across the kitchen and out the door.

"Another one? I thought the camera was my anniversary gift." Cam had tucked it in the corner of the tray when he'd served her breakfast in bed that morning.

It was hard to believe that only a year ago she and Cam had exchanged their wedding vows underneath the apple trees.

"That was from Dad," Beth said. "This one is from me and Grandma."

"Oh, oh." Julia grinned. "Then it has to be something pink."

"The bow is pink," Cam said under his breath. "Careful. Here's the step."

Her heart stirred at the protective note in his voice. "Are you worried I'll fall over?" she teased.

"You are a little off balance."

She couldn't argue with him there. Being seven months pregnant did tend to change a woman's center of gravity.

"Stop!" Beth gave the command and Julia tugged off the blindfold.

It took a moment for her to realize there was another horse in the pasture. The hollow-faced buckskin had a choppy mane and a short, broomstick tail but his halter sported a cotton candy–pink bow.

"Your mom dropped him off an hour ago. She's in the barn getting another stall ready."

Julia smiled.

Tara had come back to Jackson Lake for the wedding and surprised them all with her decision to stay. She'd claimed there was no point in the brick house standing empty after the Delaney family had unanimously voted to take up residence in the old house across the field, but Tara's bluster hadn't fooled anyone. Beth had completely won over her adopted grandmother. And since her return, Tara had become as guilty as the rest of them of rescuing animals and transplanting them to the farm.

"So, what do think, Mrs. Delaney?" Cam murmured in her ear. "Is there room for one more?"

Julia looked up at him. "Always, Mr. Delaney. Always."

"I named him Ranger, Mom," Beth said eagerly.

"He's beautiful," Julia said. "All he needs now is a clean stall and a good meal."

"And love," Beth added.

"And love."

Julia felt the warmth of Cam's arms around her and leaned into his embrace.

Thanked God there was more than enough of that to go around at Second Chance Farm.

NOTE FROM THE AUTHOR

If you enjoyed your visit to Jackson Lake, look for *Operation: Mistletoe*, another heart-warming novella that celebrates love and new beginnings (and features not one, but four, pint-sized matchmakers!) I'd love to hear from you! Sign up for my newsletter at kathryn-springer.com and you'll get a free short story, available only to subscribers. While you're there, be sure to check out my upcoming women's fiction release *The Gathering Table* from Love Inspired Trade.

ABOUT THE AUTHOR

USA Today bestselling author Kathryn Springer has written over thirty novels. She lives on a lake in northern Wisconsin and enjoys long walks in the woods and the change of seasons (although sometimes she wishes the "change" between winter and spring wouldn't last quite so long!) Kathryn loves small-town settings and stories that celebrate new beginnings and happily-ever-afters. Find out more about her books at www.kathrynspringer.com.

ALSO BY KATHRYN SPRINGER

Castle Falls (Harlequin Love Inspired™)

The Bachelor Next Door

The Bachelor's Twins

The Bachelor's Perfect Match

The Holiday Secret

Novellas

A September Bride (Autumn Brides Collection/Zondervan)

Love on a Deadline (Year of Weddings Collection/Zondervan)

Long Contemporary

The Dandelion Field

The Hearts We Mend

Made in the USA
Middletown, DE
29 November 2021